Monster Island

Monster Island

by

Freddie Alexander

Illustrated by Helen O'Higgins

HarperCollins*Ireland*

HarperCollins*Ireland*
The Watermarque Building
Ringsend Road
Dublin DO4 K7N3
Ireland

a division of
HarperCollins*Publishers*
1 London Bridge Street
London SE1 9GF
UK

www.harpercollins.co.uk

First published by HarperCollins*Ireland* in 2022

1 3 5 7 9 10 8 6 4 2

A catalogue record of this book is available from the British Library

HB ISBN 978-0-00-847315-0

Typeset in Adobe Caslon Pro by
Palimpsest Book Production Ltd, Falkirk, Stirlingshire

Printed and Bound in the UK using 100% Renewable Electricity
at CPI Group (UK) Ltd

About the Author

Freddie Alexander lives in Dublin with his wife and son. As a child, Freddie was terrified of the monsters from under the bed. These days, his snoring keeps them away. *Monster Island* is his second book

Photo by Zelda Cunningham

Helen O'Higgins is an Irish illustrator and printmaker based in Dublin. *Monster Island* is the second book she has illustrated.

Photo by Killian Broderick

For Zelda and Rafe with love

CHAPTER
1

First off, let's get one thing clear.

Monsters under the bed are real.

Let me repeat.

MONSTERS UNDER THE BED ARE REAL.

Sing it in the streets and scream it from the rooftops for all to hear.

MONSTERS UNDER THE BED ARE REAL!

Very real.

You may have been told otherwise. You may even have been told that to believe in such nonsense is silly and childish; that such creatures are a figment of your imagination. Well, let me tell you, Reader, to ignore my warning would be a mistake. And here is why . . .

There is a world under the bed that is as real as yours or mine.

It is a world of magic, both good and bad (and whoever says that magic is not real is very foolish indeed).

It is a world so different to our own, yet so similar at the same time.

It is a world with good creatures and, most definitely, very bad creatures.

And before you ask, yes, I *have* had my head examined; no, I have *not* eaten or drunk anything funny; and yes, I *am* telling you the truth. Now hush up and listen.

You see, monsters under the bed *love* children.

Not in the same way that your mum, or your dad, or your granny, or your dog, or your cat, or your goldfish loves you. No, Reader. Not at all. These monsters love children like you love . . . a large slice of chocolate cake . . . or a huge bag of sweets . . . or a large raw onion . . .

Well, perhaps not a large raw onion.

That's right, monsters under the bed love to *eat* children.

Now, before you start screaming in terror, you will be relieved to know that most of these monsters do not come from under *your* bed. Or your neighbour's bed. Or your neighbour's flower bed for that matter.

Most of these monsters come from a place which is quite a safe distance from *your* hands, and *your* fingers, and *your* feet, and *your* toes. Yes, in all likelihood, these creatures shall leave *your* toenails entirely untouched.

That is not to say that you are completely safe, Reader. So, as the old saying goes, 'sit up and pay attention, just in case'.

Now, regrettably, these horrible creatures do not just *eat* children. No. As you will learn, there is a fate worse than being a starter, a main course and a dessert all at once.

And that is this (*to be read in a whisper for added effect*): There are some monsters that can sneak inside a child at night and take over that child's body and mind. (*Back to normal indoor voice, please. Thank you.*)

I do not know why this is, Reader. There may be many reasons.

Perhaps they want to know what it is like to jump up and down on a bouncing castle at a birthday party. Or maybe they want to know what it is like to throw a paper aeroplane while a teacher is not looking. Or they might even want to know what it is like to pick a child's nose.

I could guess and guess and guess all day long. Quite simply, I do not know why precisely they would want to possess a child, but they do.

Can you imagine the horror of it? Picture it. One of these creatures munching *your* cereal, eating *your* snot, being tucked into *your* bed and *no one* would be any the wiser. Not even your cat or your dog (and they know everything).

Another thing to know about these monsters is that they *hate* grown-ups.

Not *hate* in the same way that you hate, say, home-work, or listening to some boring teacher drone on about what you must *do* for your homework, or watching a very (very) long documentary on the history of homework.

No, these monsters cannot stand the taste of grown-ups because they drink too much coffee and are filled with nothing but horrible thoughts like . . . making *you* eat your vegetables . . . or emptying the bins . . . or, 'These telephone bills are too high; no more transatlantic calls to the president of Peru for you!'

Chapter 1

In all seriousness, at this point I feel a **<u>DISCLAIMER</u>** to be appropriate. If you should find this story too scary, or if any grown-ups should find it too rude, then, by all means, please feel free to close this book and never open it again. Feed it to your goldfish with your leftovers if you like.

BUT . . .

If you want to learn more about these monsters, you should, nay, you *must* continue to read this story. For this, you will learn, is one with tips and tricks on how to deal with these grotesque and sneaky creatures on the tiniest of off chances that you ever come across one.

And if by the end of this book you are still with me in one piece, you might do me the favour of yelling for all to hear:

MONSTERS UNDER THE BED ARE REAL!

So, where to begin?

Well, first you'll need to get nice and comfy. Oh, and before you read any further, just to be absolutely safe, I suggest that if you are in bed, please ensure that, like a rollercoaster, your arms and your legs are tucked in nice and tight under your sheets and well away from the edge of the bed. This way, I would fully expect that you shall not suffer any gruesome or grisly interruptions while reading this book.

Well, we'll see.

Are you ready?

Excellent, let's go!

CHAPTER
2

This story is set many, many years ago, long before you were even born, when I was just a wee lad. How wee, you ask? Well, I'm afraid it's rude to ask grown-ups their age, so I suppose you'll never know precisely.

Did electricity exist? Yes, just about. Did the internet exist? Only if you are asking about a strange type of fishing net. Were velvet blazers in fashion? Trick question: velvet blazers are *always* in fashion, Reader.

Our story begins with Sam Shipwright, an 11-year-old girl, who did not have much in common with the other girls in her school. In fact, she hated all things 'girlie'.

She hated wearing dresses and loved fishing. She hated dolls and loved spitting. She enjoyed skipping, but only as part of her boxing training.

She was tall for her age and had thick, black hair which stopped just above her shoulders. She nearly always wore jeans, grubby runners and a trusted red hoodie.

Sam's classmates considered her a strange child (although most people I know are a bit strange). Not that she *was* strange, rather she did not fit in with the crowd. You see, Sam answered to no one. She did not fall in with the popular girls and, in turn, with the rest of the pack. Sam kept herself to herself and she was just fine with that, thank you very much.

Sam's parents too kept to themselves. And they too answered to no one. They never had guests over to their house. They never answered the telephone. And they *never* answered the front door (a good life lesson right there).

In many ways, Sam's life was perfection. Just her, her mum and her dad.

It was a very sad event that turned her life upside down and inside out.

Sam's world changed forever when she was informed of her parents' tragic passing. It does not matter how it happened, Reader. I shall spare you the details. All that you need to know right now is that Sam's life shattered into a million pieces that day. Although Sam could be described as a brave child, a tough child, this was a setback too great and she went even more inside herself.

Sam had lived in Dublin, Ireland with her parents. Maybe I should have told you this earlier, but in my defence we are still very early on in this story. Plus you never asked, so let's not argue and just move on.

Hers had been a wonderful home, there is no doubt about that. One with fancy red-brick houses and cobbled tree-lined streets. One with ponds for paddle boating and tucked away pubs for belly bloating. One with people named Bertram and Verity (you know the sort).

Sam had not known her grandad before her parents' tragic deaths. She had never met him at all, in fact. For, you see, he lived on a remote island north-west of Dublin, north-west of Ireland and, Sam would soon discover, north-west of central heating.

The island was called Draymur Isle and, in more ways than one, it was a very inconvenient place to live indeed. To put it in perspective, Reader, if you can imagine the most inconvenient place you have ever been to in your life, this was most definitely north-west of that.

Sam's first sight of Grandad was from the upstairs landing. He was just a tall silhouette standing in the front doorway. He wore a trench coat, a fishing hat and had a suitcase from the Stone Age. He carried a walking stick, using it every third step only.

From their very first meeting, Grandad took charge. He had a calm and gentle presence about him that immediately reassured and comforted her.

'Everything will be okay, my dear,' Grandad told her in his unusual accent. 'You can rely on me fully to take care of you always.'

Sam needed no further convincing. She was exhausted and so deeply hurt that these words alone convinced her.

Chapter 2

She fell into his arms – this man, who was little more than a stranger – and they cried. There was no looking back; the pair were made for each other.

From his old photographs, it was clear that Grandad had once been a very handsome man, but he had all sorts wrong with him now; mainly a bad limp that he had picked up in 'the war' (although he had been vague about *which* war). He was weary in movement and looked older than he was. He wore shirts, never t-shirts, as is normal for men above a certain age. He always smoked a pipe and spluttered heartily if he laughed too hard.

Sam learned that Grandad had left school at the age of 12. While his classmates had been inside studying history, or maths, or science, Grandad – or Jacob, as he was called back then – was outside the school gates learning about animals, and birds, and bees, and trees, and sorts. He was self-taught in every which way and was a veteran of adventure, as well as war, having travelled far and wide.

After some weeks in the red brick house, Grandad felt it right for Sam to get away from it all. It was agreed that they would return to Grandad's home on Draymur Isle. Sam put up little resistance because, in truth, she needed to be as far away from this dreaded reality as possible.

So, she packed her bags. She was sad to be leaving, but could not stay any longer.

Before she left, Sam went into her parents' room and looked in her mother's dresser. She found what she was looking for immediately: an old snow globe about the size of a tennis ball. She shook it and the globe lit up brightly. Inside stood a small lighthouse, no bigger than your thumb. The snowflakes swirled hypnotically, and her vision blurred with tears.

Sam carefully placed the snow globe into her bag pack, turned off her parents' light and left the room for the last time.

CHAPTER

3

Very, very early the next morning, they set off on the long, long journey to Draymur Isle. It was so early in fact that it was still the night before. They had taken a taxi to a bus station, where they waited for a bus, which was of course late. The bus drove them at breathtaking speed to the very north-west edge of Ireland. From there they hopped on a boat that floated for many hours across an extremely rough and vomit-inducing sea.

It was very late when they arrived on Draymur Isle which was dark, and jagged, and cold. An unkeen ferryman tossed their suitcases onto a tiny harbour and hurried the pair off. He did not stick around to take in the view either.

Chapter 3

'Welcome to Draymur Isle,' shouted Grandad above the wild weather, clasping his hat to his head for safe keeping.

The sea and the rain swept in from all angles and the two were sodden within seconds. Sam's first impression was of a harsh and unfriendly place . . . and she was right to feel uneasy.

The two made their way up to Grandad's home – a disused lighthouse, dangerously close to a cliff edge. Although she would never admit it, Sam felt nervous as she walked the dark and unsteady terrain towards her new home.

By all accounts, by which I mean, what Grandad had told Sam, the island was wildly unwelcoming for much of the year. It was often freezing and, while it was striking in its own way, it was very different to Dublin. No bright lights. No hustle and bustle. No frequent traffic jams. Hardly anyone ever came to Draymur Isle and people rarely left, so everybody knew everybody.

The lighthouse was more or less the same as it had been one hundred years earlier, except the great light was not used any more – there was no need, as boats tended to avoid the island and its ever-choppy waters altogether. There was no oven, so cooking normally took place in a heavy pot that hung over the fire. The toilet was in an outhouse next to the cliff which was, as you can imagine, Reader, unbearable during the winter months (and surprisingly pleasant during the summer months).

Grandad lived alone. Well, almost alone. He owned a whiter-than-white dairy goat named Myrtle. She was not a clever animal and spent most days eating plants, and shoes, and books, and really anything she could get her teeth on. She ate most of Grandad's belongings. But on the upside, this meant that the lighthouse had a minimal feel and was always tidy.

On entering the lighthouse upon their arrival, Myrtle stared at Sam suspiciously.

'Now, very slowly,' instructed Grandad nervously, placing a small package into her hand, 'set this cheese sandwich in front of Myrtle.'

Sam slowly placed the sandwich before the intimidating goat and bowed as Grandad had instructed on their walk from the ferry.

Myrtle considered the tinfoil-wrapped sandwich before her. She took one sniff and scoffed the sacrificial snack at an alarming speed. The goat bowed back at Sam.

Grandad let out a sigh of relief. The peace offering had been accepted and Myrtle took to Sam like a long-lost friend.

'Myrtle, this is Sam,' smiled Grandad, stroking the greedy goat's beard. 'She will be living with us from now on.'

This might all sound very strange, Reader, but Grandad's caution was not without good reason. You see, Myrtle had a violent temper and did not like anybody on the island except for Grandad. In fact, anybody who came close to their lighthouse was quickly escorted from the property, by which I mean violently chased, sprinting and screaming, by the manic goat. Nobody on Draymur Isle crossed Myrtle.

While life on the island would take some getting used to, Sam enjoyed Grandad and Myrtle's company from the start.

For one, it was immediately clear that Grandad was a fantastic storyteller. He had an aura about him that would make anyone sit up and listen. He had a unique accent and a voice that held a room's attention, so it was impossible not to hang on his every word. English was not his first language, so he had an interesting way of speaking. He built great fires too – one inside for cooking, heating and bath water, and another outside for burning rubbish (global warming had not yet been discovered).

Late at night, Grandad cooked what he liked to call 'Bedtime Supper'. Bedtime Supper commenced at around ten or eleven and usually consisted of a few sausages cooked in the heavy pot that hung over the fire. Instead of plates, they used bread, not only to avoid cleaning, but because Myrtle had eaten all the plates. This was thoroughly enjoyable and worth the late-night burping.

On Sam's very first night in the lighthouse, before she had even unpacked, they settled in front of the fire for Bedtime Supper. After Sam and Grandad had finished their sausages, and Myrtle had finished Grandad's slippers, Grandad stretched his heavy, worn legs and prepared his pipe. Sam stroked Myrtle's beard and the greedy animal snored aggressively on the floor.

'Now, you are probably tired, but I need to tell you

something very important,' said Grandad softly, making sure his pipe was packed nice and firm. 'In fact, it is probably the most important thing ever to be spoken to you.'

He took a pack of matches from his thick cardigan and lit the pipe. He had to puff it a few times to make sure that it was lit properly.

PUFF–PUFF–PUFF–PUFF

Silver smoke filled the air and Grandad let it settle before speaking. 'Have you ever heard of a creature under the bed?' he asked, leaning forward, as if eager not to be overheard.

Sam considered him for a moment. He was so close that she could see every deep wrinkle on his face; a face that reminded her of an old tree.

'Like a monster?' she replied.

'In a sense, yes.'

'Well, yeah. When I was small, people spoke about them. But they're just made up to scare children.'

Grandad let her words sink in before he spoke. 'I'm afraid that, around these parts, monsters under the bed are real and they are dangerous. Now that you are on Draymur Isle, you must learn all about them.'

Grandad suddenly stopped talking. He listened out for several moments.

'What is it, Grandad?' she asked.

The wind whirred and swirled outside but Sam felt safe with Grandad and Myrtle by the fire.

'I thought I heard something,' he replied before continuing. 'Most children don't know how to recognize the warning signs of a monster under the bed until it's too late.'

Sam smiled nervously at Grandad but he did not smile back.

'Grandad, come on, be serious.'

'Oh, I am deadly serious. I'm afraid that this island has an evil past. A *very* evil past.'

He paused to ensure that Sam was giving him her full attention.

'You see, long, long ago, this island was ruled by monsters. Terrifying, loathsome creatures that plunged the island into a grave and horrible darkness. Their reign of terror looked like it would never end; that they would torment the people here for eternity.'

'What happened?'

'It was with immense bravery that an ancient druid

of this island, one of the most powerful and magical of all people, and incidentally one of your very own ancestors, stood up to them. One day, as the legend has it, the monsters were banished at sunrise, never allowed to step foot on Draymur Isle ever again. But . . .'

Grandad took another puff or two on his pipe to keep it lit.

'But while for many years this island was at peace, the druid's protective spell started to develop cracks. Monsters began to get through once again, appearing when children were at their most vulnerable: in their beds at night.'

'But, why?' asked Sam, who struggled to believe what her grandfather was telling her.

'Why, to eat the children of this island while they sleep, of course,' he replied, as if it was perfectly obvious. 'Although they never come during the day. They cannot stand daylight, you see.'

'This is ridiculous, Grandad.'

'Like you, Sam, I did not believe in these monsters at first,' he said earnestly. 'I laughed it off when my mother told me about them when I was young. After all, there's nothing under the bed. There's nothing there. Just darkness. Or so you think.'

Grandad leaned down slowly and pulled up his right trouser leg to his knee.

Grandad's lower leg, from his knee down to his ankle, was seriously scarred. His shin was purple and blotchy and, for a moment, Sam couldn't speak. His leg was as thin as a walking stick and unfitting of the great man's build. She wondered if it was painful.

'Is that from the war, Grandad?' asked Sam eventually, quietly.

'That is the work of a splocher,' he said in a hushed tone.

'A *splocher*?' replied Sam, also keeping her voice down so that the fire crackled loudly by comparison.

'A splocher is a type of monster that comes from under the bed – a nasty, stupid, clumsy piece of work. They're very greedy and they absolutely *love* to eat children. They sneak out from under the bed in the middle of the night, sniffing for any feet, or hands, or fingers, or toes sticking out from under the covers.'

Sam studied Grandad's leg. She felt her stomach tilt, more with sadness for Grandad than anything else. She ran her fingers along the uneven scarring which reminded her of melted candle wax. His shin was so skinny that it looked more like a cane than a leg.

'I don't want this to happen again, Grandad,' she looked up at him. 'To you, I mean.'

'Ha!' he laughed without humour. 'I am more worried for you.'

'Will you teach me about them? The . . . *splochers*?'

Grandad relit his pipe.

'I will, surely, my dear.' He smiled. 'I will tell you about all of the monsters that come from under the bed. As I said before, you can rely on me fully to take care of you always.'

Sam was not sure if Grandad was pulling her leg. Still, he was a great storyteller and, just to be on the safe, she listened very carefully.

CHAPTER
4

'Splochers love to eat children,' said Grandad.

Sam sat wide eyed in front of the fire.

'They are incredibly greedy,' he continued. 'Pigs, the lot of them. They look more like large slugs with snouts, except they prefer chomping at children's hands and feet rather than lettuce heads. They sludge across the floorboards, leaving a strange, silky green juice as they go. They've got no arms or legs, so they can't actually get up very high from under the bed. In fact, they're quite clumsy in their movement. But they're born with a distinct . . . skill.'

'Skill?' asked Sam quietly.

'Unlike most predators, like lions, or crocodiles, or anteaters—'

'Anteaters?'

'Yes, haven't you heard of an anteater before? I should explain: they eat ants – like the insect, not aunts like your Great Aunt Rita.'

'Of course I know what an anteater is! But they're not dangerous.'

'Well, maybe to *you* they're not dangerous, but to ants they are treacherous . . . Do you know any ants?'

'No, but–'

'Exactly. They are incredibly effective predators. Now, where was I?'

'You were saying, "Unlike most predators".'

'Ah, yes, *most* predators,' said Grandad in his hushed and hoarse voice, 'have arms, or legs, or claws, or fins and can pounce, or spring, or swoop, but not a splocher. A splocher is different because they are just like great big violent balls of snot without any way to push or pull themselves up.'

'Well, what do they do?'

'They have a good, gassy leap in them. Their stomachs gurgle and gargle as they sneak around under the bed and, when they feel the time is right, an explosion out their backside *thrusts* them into the air and they snatch their bite.'

'Like a fart.'

'A *fart*? I don't know this word *fart*. What does *fart* mean?'

Sam thought for a moment. 'It doesn't matter, Grandad.'

He threw a sod of turf onto the fire and continued. 'They only have one good leap in them; it takes a lot of energy, but they nearly always take their chance.'

Grandad put both hands together to form the shape of a splocher biting.

'Snap!' he whispered, clasping his hands shut. 'Splochers have a huge collection of horrible, spiky teeth, so that once they have you, well, it won't be pretty.'

'This can't be true! If it were, why doesn't everyone know about splochers? I mean, if they're attacking children from under the bed, surely grown-ups would do something?'

'That's just it. Grown-ups don't believe in them.'

'What? But look at your leg, Grandad!'

Chapter 4

Grandad let out a weary sigh. 'Grown-ups cannot see the wounds left by a splocher, or any marks left by any of these monsters for that matter. Unless of course they were attacked by one as a child. Then you'd never forget, believe you me.'

Sam sat frozen beside the fire. Myrtle let out a sudden snort from her slumber that made Sam jump.

'They speak a strange language called Grimmlish,' continued Grandad, rolling his trouser leg back down to cover his mutilated shin. 'It's like a type of broken English. All they talk about is eating children – or *crimmplers* as they call them.'

'Crimmplers?'

'That's right – it means *children*. All day long, all they talk about is crunching, munching, chewing, and chomping crimmplers. Quite grim, so their language is called Grimmlish.'

'Is there nothing that can be done to stop them?' asked Sam.

'Well, actually, there is one thing . . . one thing that makes them think twice before making a move. Jam.'

'What?'

'Splochers hate jam. Do not ask me why, but they simply cannot stand the stuff.'

'But . . . *jam?*'

'I know, it is very strange. Haven't you wondered why I have so much jam smeared everywhere in here?'

Sam had thought it strange, but her parents had raised her not to point out odd and quirky character traits.

'I thought it rude to ask,' she replied.

'It's to keep the splochers away.'

Grandad got to his feet, picking up his walking stick as he rose. He moved slowly across the room, his shoes making sticking noises as he went. The living area was all one room with an armchair and a fireplace on one side, and a humble kitchen with a small table and a few chairs on the other. The walls and floor were made of stone, but it felt cosy.

Grandad opened a cupboard door above the kitchen sink which was absolutely jammed (no pun intended, Reader) with nothing but jar after jar of jam. *This* was an impressive collection of jam in and of itself, but then he opened all the cupboards under the sink and these *too* were full of jam. Next, he hobbled across to the front door to three old wicker baskets that Sam had assumed stored peat or turf or coal for the fire. But these *three* were full of jam! Lastly, Grandad got down on all fours and crobbled (note: a mix between a crawl and a hobble) under the kitchen table to reveal a trapdoor that led to an underground pantry. And guess what was inside?

Cabbage.

Only joking, Reader – that's right, it was full to the brim with a seemingly endless supply of jars *full* of jam!

Grandad began to list his large collection of jams enthusiastically. 'I've got raspberry jam, strawberry jam, liver and kidney jam . . .'

'Liver and kidney jam!'

'Well, I get tired of fruit jams all the time. Where was I? Ah yes . . . Brussels sprout jam. Boiled rat jam. Old shoelace jam. So long as it's jam, it's in here.'

Sam looked a shade of lime-green jam.

'To be safe,' suggested Grandad, picking out a jar of shepherd's pie jam, 'I would eat at least three jars of jam every day.'

Sam nodded reluctantly.

'*And*, I would make sure that your hands and feet are smeared in jam before you go to bed.'

'Is that really necessary?' asked Sam.

Grandad began to pull up his trouser leg once more.

'All right, all right! Any other monsters I should know about?" asked Sam (a question she never thought she would ask).

Grandad closed the cupboard doors carefully. He made his way back to the fire, the sticking sound following him as he walked.

'Unfortunately,' he said as he sat back down, 'there are worse monsters than splochers.'

'Worse?' exclaimed Sam. 'How can there be anything worse than a splocher that wants to eat your toes while you sleep?'

Chapter 4

Grandad smiled thoughtfully, resting the pipe on his lower lip.

'The next monster under the bed which you absolutely, most desperately need to know about is called a serpentail.'

'A *serpentail*?'

'Serpentails are like long vines that crawl up the sides of buildings, or like snakes without a mouth.'

'They don't sound too bad,' said Sam, trying to put on a brave face.

Grandad laughed heartily before spluttering tremendously.

'Serpentails, in my opinion, are the sneakiest of the monsters. They slink up under the covers and wring you like you might wring a sponge,' whispered Grandad, using a tea towel gripped in his grasp to illustrate his point. 'They like to guzzle a child's blood like a refreshing glass of prune juice. Do you drink prune juice?'

Sam sat back, aghast and shook her head silently.

'Don't look so shocked – everyone should drink prune juice. You know the old saying, "A glass of prune juice a day keeps constipation at bay." I used to make my own prunes, you know. I held the world record for the world's most wrinkly prune.'

'Are the serpentails afraid of jam too?'

'Ha, don't be ridiculous!'

'Well, is there anything that can stop a serpentail, then?' urged Sam.

'Laughter. Children's laughter to be precise. Now, that may sound straightforward, but it's anything but.'

Grandad paused to take a sip from the water in his hip flask and treated Myrtle to a drop. The bearded goat slumped happily.

'Imagine being all cosy and dreamy in your bed when suddenly you wake up to find yourself being guzzled down by a serpentail,' he continued. 'You wouldn't much feel like laughing like you mean it, would you? And you *must* laugh like you mean it.'

Sam could not believe what she was hearing.

'A serpentail moves at lightning speed when needs must. When it wants to, it acts so fast that there will be no sound for anyone to hear.'

Sam was appropriately startled.

'So, if you ever find yourself faced with a serpentail, you better laugh quickly, because, once they get their suckers into you, you're mincemeat to them. Or prune juice, more accurately.'

'But why do they fear children's laughter?'

'Because it represents a child's joy, a sound that no serpentail can bear."

Sam thought carefully for a few moments.

'So all I need to do is cover myself in jam and laugh if I see a serpentail. I can do that. Anything else?'

Grandad looked into the fire, like he was having one of those moments when you're caught by a gaze and you don't want to break the stare.

'There is one more creature I need to warn you about. Worse than a splocher and worse than a serpentail,' he said, his voice hushed and hoarse once more.

'A *silentrap*, Sam, is the worst of all the monsters from under the bed. Actually,' considered Grandad, the reflection of the fire flickering in his faraway eyes, 'a silentrap is the worst monster that has ever existed.'

Sam's stomach lurched. She spoke not a word but waited patiently.

Grandad suddenly looked her straight in the eyes.

'While a splocher dines on your toes and fingers, and a serpentail squeezes you prune dry, these attacks are telling for all children to see.

'A silentrap, however, rests in the shadows. Nobody knows exactly what a silentrap looks like because nobody has ever properly seen one. Maybe they could be best described as black shadows that seep from under the bed. Black shadows that wisp through walls and disappear in the wind without a trace.'

Sam darted suspicious glances at the different shadows on the walls.

'A silentrap does not want to nibble at your toes or drain you dry. No, it is the child's soul that the silentrap will consume; that is what fuels it. A silentrap will bide its time, selecting its victim carefully. A child's soul is a very powerful thing, you see, and could keep a silentrap satisfied for a long time. Maybe that explains why they so rarely appear. But don't be fooled, they are the very worst of the monsters.

'For you see, a silentrap will take over a child so much that eventually, over time, not even the child's nearest and dearest will recognize any part of him or her. As for what happens to the *real* child within, I am not so sure.' Grandad paused, his breath shaking. 'A silentrap is the very essence of evil, Sam.'

'How do you know all this, Grandad?' asked Sam quietly.

Not a word was spoken for a long minute as Grandad ignored her question. He seemed in a trance as the wind whirred and whistled through the cracks and crevasses of the lighthouse outside.

A log *CRACKED* in the flames and he snapped from his daze.

'Not only is a silentrap hard to spot, but it is nearly impossible to hear because it can camouflage its noise.'

'How do you mean?' asked Sam timidly.

The two now spoke very softly. So softly as if to keep their conversation secret from the shadows.

'A silentrap sounds like the environment that a child is in. So it could make the noise of a train passing in the night, or the banging of the pipes, or the barking of a dog outside, or a car alarm in the distance, or the wisping of the wind and the crashing of the waves.'

Grandad took off his glasses and mopped his teary eyes.

'Are you okay, Grandad?'

Grandad seemed lost for a moment before suddenly clearing his throat.

'I'm fine,' he said, composing himself gruffly. 'Not only can a silentrap camouflage *its* sound, but it can also camouflage a child's voice too. So if a child is yelling or screaming, a silentrap can make this sound like a sneeze, or a storm, or the birds chirping to an adult.'

'But . . . isn't there any way to stop them?'

'Well, there is one thing. While it does not defeat a silentrap, it can help a child discover its presence.'

'What is it?' asked Sam, her hand on Grandad's.

'A silentrap can trick you into thinking whatever grown-up is in the next room is calling you. They are incredible at impersonations.'

'But, why?' considered Sam.

'I'm not sure. The only reason I can think of is to make the child an easier target. If a parent calls their child to come to them, the child will get up out of the bed and a silentrap can sweep in from the shadows and possess their soul quicker. That is why it is very important if anyone calls you in the night to stay in your bed under the covers. No matter what.'

36

'If they are so good at impersonations, how would I know that it's a silentrap calling and not you?'

'Excellent question, Sam. Nicknames.'

'Nicknames?'

'We shall have nicknames for one another so if I do need to call you at night it shall be by your nickname, not *Sam*, or anything else.'

'Oh, how about I call you–'

'Stop!' interrupted Grandad. 'You never know if the shadows are listening. We are never alone on this island.'

Grandad took a small notepad from his cardigan and scribbled down his nickname for Sam. He shielded it as best he could so that Sam had to peer in between his hands to read it:

MYRTLE'S BEARD.

'Now, you write down a nickname for me.'

Sam took the notepad and wrote on it before shielding it so only Grandad could see:

CANE.

37

'Grandad, how do you know all this?' asked Sam, determined to find out more.

Grandad thought before answering.

'I've had a lot of experience with these monsters, my dear,' he said, standing. 'Just remember the nicknames and only move from your bed during the night if I call you by that name. I mean that, Sam.'

Grandad threw the paper into the fire so that it was quickly engulfed by flames.

'Now, you have your first day of school tomorrow and unfortunately it is time for bed.'

For some reason, Reader, Sam did not feel like going to bed in the slightest.

CHAPTER
5

SQUELCH – SQUISH – SQUELCH – SQUISH – SQUELCH . . .

Sam's room was at the very top of the old lighthouse. As she nervously climbed the spiral stone stairway, she felt as though she had stepped back in time. It was dark and her feet were bare except for the very generous helping of rhubarb jam smeared all between her toes, causing her feet to stick horribly to the floor with a SQUELCH – SQUISH – SQUELCH – SQUISH – SQUELCH . . .

Sam opened the door to her room, which took a moment as it was jammed shut (not by jam, but because the door was so old and rickety).

The room was circular with little more than a single

bed to one side and a chest of drawers to the other. This used to be where light signals were sent to guide passing ships and the wall was almost entirely windowpane, from the floor right up to the ceiling.

Sam heaved her suitcase up the last step and plonked it inside next to the bedroom door. She peered out the window and, although it was dark, she could still make out the white waves as they crashed heavily against the cliff face directly below. The moon, which lit the ever stormy sweeping waters, was a stark contrast to the jagged blackness of the cliff face.

Although Sam could be described as brave, she got into bed immediately. She even ensured that the sheets were tightly tucked in, and that her arms and feet remained firmly inside the covers. While Grandad's warnings seemed very far-fetched, she was on edge.

Sam lay nervously, watching her warm breath cloud above her face. She stared at the ceiling and examined the large contraption straight above. It was enormous and Sam realized it had been used to hold the powerful light bulbs required to guide passing ships through the stormy seas. But not any more.

Chapter 5

Sam spotted a picture frame on the chest of drawers by her bed. She could make out two figures standing in the picture. She squinted but could not make out who they were from here.

Curiosity got the better of her and, for just a moment (rather remarkably if you ask me), she forgot about the splochers, and the serpentails, and the silentraps. She tippy-toed across the creaky floorboards and peered at the frame. It was a black and white photograph of two boys: one tall, the other short. They were grinning from ear to ear as they held up an enormous fish. In fact, they appeared to be laughing.

Then came a sudden shout.

'Sam!'

Sam darted back to her bed, leaping under the covers. 'Grandad?' she called.

'SAM!' yelled Grandad's voice again. It came from just outside her door.

'Grandad, what is it?'

Grandad sounded in pain. 'Sam! I've had a fall. My leg . . . I think it's broken!'

Sam pushed back the covers but hesitated before

getting out of bed. *Remember, silentraps are incredible at impersonations.*

'What's my nickname, Grandad?'

'OOOOWWWW!' wailed Grandad. 'Sam, please! I've no time for that! Help me!'

Grandad sounded in a lot of pain, but Sam stayed put.

'I'll come and help, Grandad . . . Just call me by my nickname first, like you told me to!'

There was quiet.

'Sam, help me!' cried Grandad again. 'I've never felt pain as bad as this in all my life!'

Sam heard Grandad scream in agony once more. She could not take it. She pushed back the covers, hopped from her bed and swung open the bedroom door.

SWOOSH!

Sam was knocked to the floor. She was dazed and struggled to focus on the shapes in front of her. Her heart pounded and for a moment she was too frightened to even scream. Then she recognized the fishing net covering her face.

'Grandad!'

Grandad was covered from head to toe in blackcurrant jam, which acted as a camouflage as well as a splocher deterrent.

'Why did you get out of bed, Sam?' exclaimed Grandad.

'What are you doing, Grandad?' screamed Sam, feeling at least triple her age. 'I nearly jumped out of my skin!'

'I had to test you! Look,' said Grandad sitting up on the floor slowly, Myrtle licking the jam from his face. 'You must do exactly what I say, because if that was a real silentrap calling, it could have possessed you all too easily. Do you understand me, Sam?'

Sam was about to argue but saw the fear in Grandad's eyes. From what Grandad had told her about silentraps, staying in or out of bed seemed irrelevant. Still, it mattered to him and so it mattered to Sam.

'I'm sorry, Grandad. I won't get out of bed until morning without the nickname.'

Grandad tucked Sam in and hobbled out of the room.

Sam listened to his sticky steps (and Myrtle's sticky hooves) descend the stone stairway.

It had been a long day and Sam was exhausted. Although now fittingly paranoid about the monsters under the bed, eventually she could fight the fight no more and sleep took her.

CHAPTER
6

The sun had just risen but it was clear that Grandad had been up for some time.

The fire was already burning and steaming porridge jam hung in a black pot over the flames. The steaming porridge jam looked remarkably like normal porridge, although Grandad seemed to be making a point of saying 'jam' aloud in case any splochers happened to be listening.

'Now, my dear!' yelled Grandad clearly, 'make sure you have plenty of hot porridge *JAM*, it's a cold one out there today and you've a fair walk ahead of you, so plenty of *JAM* for you! Who doesn't love a good helping of *JAM*!'

Sam was less interested in the jam and more interested

in locating her shoes, but she could not find them anywhere.

'Grandad?'

'Now,' continued Grandad. 'I've made you some jam sandwiches for lunch, and there's also some chocolate digestive biscuit jam there too.'

'Grandad!'

'You don't like chocolate digestive biscuit jam?' asked Grandad.

'Have you seen my shoes anywhere?' asked Sam.

Grandad eyed Myrtle immediately.

'No, no, I'm certain I brought them upstairs with me last night,' said Sam. 'They were beside my bed after you and Myrtle left.'

'Hmm. Well, you can borrow my fishing boots until they show up,' replied Grandad, handing Sam his boots which were at least six sizes too big for her.

'I can't wear these – they're too big!'

'You'll grow into them,' said Grandad. 'Now, I've got some work to do. You better get going or you'll be late.'

Grandad pushed her out the open front door, handed her the packed lunch, and closed the door in her face.

Chapter 6

'Where's the school though?' called Sam, nursing her nose.

'You're a smart girl, you'll find it,' called Grandad through the closed door. 'Good luck, Sam!'

The weather was biting so Sam quickly put on Grandad's fishing boots.

It had been dark when they'd arrived the night before, and so this was Sam's first chance to take in her new home properly. She had not slept particularly well – what with the thoughts of monsters wanting to eat her – and Grandad's sweaty fishing boots were sticking to her bare feet like damp seaweed. Still though, it was a bright autumnal morning, the air was fresh, and her fingers and toes were all accounted for.

After removing the seaweed from Grandad's fishing boots, an educated guess told her that the school was not off the sharp cliff behind the lighthouse, and so she had only one direction to go – towards the small village.

Sam walked for a few minutes across a field or two, or three, before joining an old grass road which had obviously been mostly used by tractors. She felt nervous as she paced. Sam had never much cared what other children thought of her, but starting a new school in a new place was daunting even to her.

She passed a small number of scattered houses as she entered the outskirts of the village, which looked pretty in the morning light. As she passed one particularly thatched house, the front door opened and out stormed a scruffy blond-haired boy in need of a good haircut. He was about Sam's age, although not as tall, and wore a white overcoat.

'Don't you walk away from me!' shouted a stocky, red-faced man who was running out after the boy. The man wore a stripy red-and-white apron over his own white overcoat.

The boy stopped at his gate and turned back.

'I don't want to be a butcher, Dad!' yelled the boy.

'You're a Hatchet and all Hatchets are butchers!' shouted the man from his front door, waving a large hatchet in the air. 'My mother was a butcher, and her father was a butcher, and *his* father was a butcher, and *his* father didn't want to become a butcher, just like *you*, and you know what happened to *him*?'

'What?' asked the boy.

'He was *butchered*!' yelled the man.

Chapter 6

The boy gasped.

'That's right, *butchered*, by which I mean sent to a military school for children who refuse to become butchers! So if you don't straighten up and butcher right, I'm getting you a one-way ticket to *Butcher Billy's Butcher Academy for Butchering Children*!'

'I am never going to be a butcher like you, you hear me! NEVER!' yelled the boy angrily, slamming his white coat to the ground and storming away towards the village.

Sam did not particularly want to speak to the reluctant trainee butcher, but she did need to find the school.

'Excuse me,' she called, walking briskly after him.

The boy stopped in his stride.

'Who are you?' asked the boy suspiciously. 'I haven't seen you around here before. Why are your feet so big?'

'Eh, I'm Sam,' she replied. 'I live in the lighthouse with my grandad.'

'Oh, I know your grandad,' replied the boy. 'My father says he's barking mad.'

Sam did not like hearing badly about Grandad and used some exotic swear words to express this fact. She stomped off towards the village.

'No, wait, I'm sorry,' called the boy as he caught up

with her. 'My father can be a right bull when he wants to be. I'm not much fond of him sometimes to be honest with you.'

Sam deliberated. 'What was that row about?' she asked.

'My dad owns the butcher shop in the village. I come from a long line of butchers, but I hate the idea of it all.'

'What do you mean?'

'Killing animals. I hate the idea of hacking them up – it's barbaric.'

The two stood for a moment.

'I'm sorry, I didn't mean to get off on the wrong foot,' said the boy before holding out his hand. 'My name is Horace. Horace Hatchet.'

Sam looked at the boy's hand, then his apologetic face.

'I'm Sam,' she said, grabbing his hand firmly. 'Grandad's Sam.'

Horace smiled. 'Are you going to the school?' he asked.

'Yes,' replied Sam.

'What age are you?'

'Eleven.'

Chapter 6

'Me too,' said Horace, smiling. 'You'll be in my class. Although . . .'

'Although *what*?' asked Sam.

'Our teacher, Major Chase, he's new. He's a nasty sort – he used to be in the army and it must have taken its toll. Bit of a drill sergeant. Or a drill *major*, I should say. He treats the class like it's a military training camp. Oh, and he's also the island's dentist.'

'The teacher *and* the dentist?'

'It's a small island, most people have two jobs,' explained Horace. 'Anyway, Major Chase is horrible. Whenever you're late or talk out of turn, he insists on giving your teeth a firm inspection there and then, which usually involves a few fillings drilled or a couple of teeth out. Terrible waste of class time and teeth if you ask me.'

The two walked into the village along an old cobbled road. This was the main street and one of the only real roads on the island. All the shops seemed to form part of someone's home.

'Mrs Barber owns the grocery shop – a nice lady,' explained Horace as they ambled along. A round and cheerful lady swept dust and flower petals from her doorway.

'Morning, Mrs Barber,' Horace called as he waved.

'Good morning, Horace. Could I interest you in a haircut today?' she asked.

'Not today, thanks, Mrs Barber!' replied Horace, then to Sam he said, 'She's also one quarter of the island barbershop. Her husband and two children make up the barbershop quartet – they sing while they trim. Next there's the post office, then we have the pub, and lastly, my dad's butcher shop. Oh, and the church and school are down here on the left.'

Horace told Sam all about himself as they walked to the school. In fact, there was no stopping him. He threatened to derail this book completely, Reader.

'I've lived here all my life, I have. My family is obsessed with being butchers. All they talk about all day is butchering meat or cooking meat. Butterflying, or mincing, or cubing, or broiling, or pan frying, or grilling, or braising, or roasting or . . . well you get the idea. But I've no interest in cutting or cooking up innocent sheep, or cattle, or dogs–'

'Dogs!' blurted Sam.

'I mean, what did they do to deserve it?' continued Horace casually, ignoring the interruption.

Chapter 6

'Well, what do you want to be if not a butcher, then?' asked Sam.

'I want to be a chef,' said Horace, smiling proudly, 'but one that's nothing to do with killing or cooking defenceless animals. I'm going to open a restaurant someday too. Want to know what I'll call it?'

'What?' asked Sam, as they passed by the church and turned into the schoolyard.

'The Meet House.'

'But I thought you won't be cooking meat?'

'I won't, it's spelled *M-E-E-T*. It's where everyone will *meet*.'

'Won't people get confused?' asked Sam.

'I don't see how.'

As Sam and Horace argued over the name of Horace's restaurant, the old church bell began to sound, which signalled the start of the school day.

'Time to go in, quick, Sam – we don't want to be late,' warned Horace, suddenly sprinting away. Sam followed her new friend inside the school quickly.

Their classroom was filled with dashing children (and I'm not talking about their looks, Reader), trying to get to their seats before the teacher arrived.

'Quick, Sam,' Horace called. 'Over here!'

The two sat at the back of the classroom, and just in time too, as in marched Major Chase.

Major Chase wore a black cape over a tweed three-piece suit. His haircut and moustache were trimmed to perfection (a big fan of barbershop quartets, thought Sam). He was quite tall with a swagger and smirk. Sam noticed him holding a shiny silver set of pliers in his right hand as he entered.

'Atteeeen-**tion!**' he yelled abruptly, and the class stood up straight like soldiers in military formation.

Sam quickly followed Horace's lead and stood up, back straight, eyes forward.

The teacher produced a list and began to call the class roll.

'Baker!' he yelled.

'Here,' a girl's hand raised at the front.

'Cheeseman!'

'Here.'

'Fisher!'

54

Chapter 6

'Here.'

And so it went on until Major Chase neared the end of the list.

'Shipwright! Wait, Shipwright? Who is Shipwright?'

Sam raised her hand. 'Here, sir. My name is Sam Shipwright.'

Major Chase glared at Sam. 'Well, don't look so terrified, Shipwright. Give us a smile.'

Sam smiled a full set of teeth and Major Chase almost licked his lips.

'You will learn that I run a tight ship, Shipwright. Best to stay on the right side of me,' advised Major Chase, glancing down fondly at the silver pliers in his hand.

With that, the door burst open and a worried-looking boy fell in through the door. His head was weighed down by a large set of second-hand braces (which, Horace later explained, Major Chase had found in the boot of his car, which also contained a small collection of war memorabilia and weaponry). Apparently, the braces were for straightening teeth but they reminded Sam more of a goalkeeper's hockey mask.

'Weaver! You are *late*!' yelled Major Chase with a bark.

'I'm sorry, sir,' spoke Weaver awkwardly through his really horrendous braces.

'We all know what happens to latecomers.'

Weaver let out a sigh and stepped forward. He opened his mouth and Major Chase began to inspect the boy's teeth.

'Let's see here. Oh, a bit too much plaque for my liking ... Broccoli for breakfast, was it Weaver?' muttered Major Chase, pulling out a pair of rubber gloves from his pocket.

What followed was some highly questionable dentistry work. The class stared down at their times tables while Major Chase assaulted the poor boy's teeth.

'How often do you brush, Weaver?' asked Major Chase enthusiastically.

''ix 'imes a 'ay, 'ir,' replied Weaver from Major Chase's homemade dentist's chair, his jaw locked open wide.

'Six, you say,' said the decorated war hero. 'We have a joker in our midst, class. Fan of limericks, are we, Weaver? How about:

There once was a boy named Walt Weaver,
When late, his teacher was no pleaser;
He opened his jaw,
And guess what he sawed;
No more wisdom teeth for poor, young Weaver!

A work in progress, Weaver, just like your timekeeping. Now, where's my chisel . . . '

Despite these alarming teaching techniques, Sam was distracted by Grandad's warnings of the previous night.

'Hey, Horace,' whispered Sam. 'Have you ever heard of monsters under the bed?'

Sam was not expecting much of a reaction, but Horace went completely pale.

He sat silently.

Sam was confused. Something was up.

For a moment, she thought he may not have heard, so she tried again. 'Have you ever heard of monsters under the bed, Horace?'

'Are you trying to get our teeth pulled out, Sam?' he asked abruptly.

'What? Seriously, what's the deal with this island and monsters under the bed?'

'Keep your voice down!' plead-whispered Horace.

Two children sitting in front of them, twins, a boy and a girl with dark hair, swivelled around.

'Excuse me. Did I hear you say that monsters under the bed are real?' the girl quietly mocked.

'That's what I heard, Ivy,' said the boy, grinning.

'Are you five years old?' pressed Ivy. 'What do you think, Wesley?'

'Pretty big feet for a five-year-old! Hey, do you believe in the Boogeyman too?' teased Wesley.

Ivy snorted laughter.

Sam's blood began to simmer.

'What's going on back there?' shouted Major Chase, incising one of Weaver's incisors. 'Hatchet, Gardiner twins, Shipwright: DETENTION AFTER SCHOOL!'

CHAPTER
7

A t three o'clock, the old church bell chimed.

'Right, class. For homework, three hundred press ups, two hundred sit ups and one hour of flossing,' ordered Major Chase.

The class groaned as they left the room, partly because of their homework assignment, partly because of their inexpertly-drilled fillings.

'You four,' roared Major Chase, 'front and centre!'

Sam, Horace, Ivy, and Wesley scurried to the front of the room and stood to attention.

Major Chase marched back and forth in front of them, his silver pliers glistening in the autumn sunshine.

'Now, then. Hatchet, please explain to Shipwright what happens when someone is caught talking in this classroom!' screamed Major Chase. (You may have noticed, Reader, that Major Chase did not have 'an indoor voice'.)

Horace stalled.

'Come on now, Hatchet!'

'A tooth out,' replied Horace.

'*A tooth out* is cor-rect, Hatchet! Well done. Mouths open, all of you!'

The four pupils opened their mouths wide for Major Chase to inspect. He tutted as he examined the line-up. 'This just won't do. Awful brushing, just awful. Let's start with . . . Shipwright!'

Major Chase spun towards Sam. He grinned a film star smile and raised the pliers to her mouth.

By some miracle, at that very moment the door opened. In came an older man, he, too, wore a black cape and a tweed suit (although his was quite baggy). He had fluffy white hair, rosy-red cheeks and he shuffled into the room with an air of nonchalance. He wore spectacles that were coloured a faint orange, presumably to protect his cataracts from the sharp autumnal light.

Major Chase jumped stiff to attention, his neck craning backwards as a mark of respect.

'Good afternoon, head-master, sir!' he declared, saluting his superior and staring straight ahead like the perfect soldier.

'Good afternoon, Major Chase,' said the Head-master with a smile. 'How are you today?'

'Very well, head-master, sir!'

Major Chase kept his eyes forward, his back impossibly straight.

The headmaster strolled around the room, pottering about casually with his hands behind his back, just as he might do in his own living room. He looked out the window at the changing leaves.

'Fine day, just fine,' he said before turning and smiling kindly at the four children. 'What is Major Chase teaching you about today?'

The headmaster stood between the teacher and the

pupils. Major Chase locked eyes with them threateningly over the headmaster's shoulder.

'Oh, em,' – began Horace – 'Major Chase was explaining some homework we didn't understand.'

'Ah, splendid!' The headmaster beamed. 'Always good to iron out the creases . . . '

Then he droned on aimlessly for a time until everyone's eyes glazed over. He may as well have been talking in Latin about paperclips. Eventually, he turned to assess Sam.

'You, dear, you're new?'

'Yes, headmaster. My name is Sam Shipwright,' replied Sam.

'She lives in the lighthouse,' added Horace.

'Ah yes,' nodded the headmaster slowly. 'Well, Sam, you are most very welcome.'

'Thank you, headmaster.'

'Now,' and the headmaster turned to face Major Chase, 'I think, it being after three o'clock, the children can head home. Don't you agree, Major Chase?'

'Yes, headmaster, *sir*!' Eyes, again, straight ahead. Posture, as always, impeccable; although Sam could sense his disappointment.

Chapter 7

The four children required no further invitation and ran into the school yard, Sam and Horace walking ahead while Ivy and Wesley ambled behind.

'*Sam* believes in monsters under the bed, did you hear that, Wesley?' exclaimed Ivy loudly so that their other classmates could hear. The school was a very small one with only a few classes, there was no more than maybe thirty pupils altogether, but all of a sudden, with all the staring, it felt like quite a large number.

'Leave her alone, Ivy,' snapped Horace.

'Oh, shall we leave your *girlfriend* alone, Horace?' teased Wesley.

'I'm warning you!' said Horace.

But Wesley kept going. 'Oh, is your *girlfriend* going to unleash the monsters under the bed?'

The twins laughed cruelly.

Horace's fists clenched and he stepped forward, but Sam held him back. The two new friends walked away as the twins shouted and wolf-whistled after them.

'Do you like jam, Horace?' asked Sam.

* * *

Sam and Horace walked back towards the old lighthouse on the cliff edge. On their way back, Sam explained everything her Grandad had told her.

'Have you ever heard of a splocher, Horace?' asked Sam.

'A *splocher*?' asked Horace.

'They're a type of monster that comes from under the bed, apparently,' explained Sam. 'My grandad says they're like massive slugs with a thousand teeth that want to eat you while you sleep.'

Horace looked down as he walked.

'What's wrong?' asked Sam.

'Cow poo,' said Horace as Sam walked Grandad's right fishing boot into a large cow pat.

'Ugh,' grimaced the city girl.

'Look, Sam,' said Horace quietly, watching her drag her boot from the enormous heap of manure, 'people around here are sensitive about . . . monsters under the bed.'

'What did you say?' she asked. 'Speak up.'

'I said that people around here are sensitive about–' He looked all around the field before again muttering, 'Monsters under the bed.'

'I still can't hear you, Horace.'

'Monsters under the bed!' he yelled.

Sam smiled. 'So you have heard of them.'

'Look, Draymur Isle is a weird place,' explained Horace, looking over his shoulder. 'It's not like anywhere else in the world. Strange things have happened here.'

'What strange things?' quizzed Sam.

The wind picked up and the rain began to spit.

'Never mind,' said Horace uneasily. 'Just be careful what you say around here, that's all. Let's keep going.'

The two crossed the last field before the lighthouse. Grandad stood in the doorway with Myrtle by his side.

'Hi, Grandad.'

'Who is your friend?' asked Grandad suspiciously.

'This is Horace. Horace Hatchet.'

Myrtle's ears pricked at the word Hatchet. Horace's father had quite the reputation. The goat began to growl aggressively like a guard dog.

'Easy, girl,' said Grandad. He rubbed Myrtle's head with his left hand and held her by the scruff of the neck with his right.

Horace looked nervous and glanced at the gate at the other side of the field.

65

'I wouldn't run,' advised Grandad. '*Hatchet*. You're a butcher.'

'Well,' began a terrified Horace, his eyes firmly on the tugging Myrtle. 'Yes, my father is Herbert Hatchet. But I don't want to be a butcher!'

'Is that so?' asked Grandad, as Myrtle struggled wildly to attack the boy.

'It's true, Grandad,' interrupted Sam. 'He hates the idea of butchering animals. He wants to be a chef.'

'A chef?' asked Grandad. 'And what will you cook if not meat, then?'

Myrtle growled louder, her milky teeth foaming.

'Eh, vegetables, maybe. Definitely *not* goat,' yelled Horace, who was frozen to the spot.

'Your father has given me a lot of stick over the years, Hatchet,' said Grandad firmly.

'Well, I'm not like my father at all, sir. He's a brute.'

Grandad considered Horace as Myrtle looked to be too strong for the old age pensioner.

'Very well,' said Grandad abruptly. 'Come on in for tea, won't you, Hatchet?'

'Better give her this,' muttered Sam, handing Horace

a packet of cheese and onion crisps (a goat's favourite type of crisps, in case you ever wondered), 'and don't forget to bow.'

Horace followed Sam's instructions and Myrtle devoured the entire packet of crisps in seconds. The goat begrudgingly bowed back at Horace, who breathed a sigh of relief.

With that, Grandad let go of the goat's neck, turned and walked inside. A reluctant Myrtle followed but eyed the nervous boy suspiciously.

On entering, Horace's jaw nearly hit the floor.

Now, do you remember Grandad said that he had work to do, Reader? Well, he had decided to take his guardianship of Sam very seriously, and spread jam on every piece of furniture, all around the sitting room.

The chairs. The table. The doormat. The cups. The spoons. The coal. The candles. Sam's toothbrush. ALL covered in jam.

Sam and Horace's feet were now completely covered in the stuff, right up over their ankles.

'Grandad, what have you done?' asked Sam, whose face was now a shade of bright raspberry jam.

'Just a precaution, my dear.'

He had even smeared jam onto the existing jam, making it jammier than ever. Sam's reputation as the mad man's granddaughter was nearly sealed in jam.

Grandad walked slowly across the room to his chair by the fire, his large frame limping somewhat.

SQUEEEEEEEELCH–SHCLOP!

SQUEEEEEEEELCH–SHCLOP!

SQUEEEEEEEELCH–SHCLOP!

Horace hunched down and dipped his finger in the jam on the floor. He sniffed it, then tasted.

For a moment his face was stony. That is, until the flavour hit his taste buds.

'*Cucumber* jam?' cried Horace, beaming, before dipping another finger into the coal bucket, which was full of dark jam.

'Dark chocolate jam!' he exclaimed (it was in fact coal jam, but coal and dark chocolate taste quite similar).

Horace began to sludge around the place, tasting the unusual variety of jam smeared all around the unusual variety of room.

'Egg salad jam . . . mashed potato jam . . . tomato soup jam . . . this is incredible!'

He began to grab big handfuls of jam, slapping them into his mouth. He was soon slathered in the stuff.

'Yorkshire pudding jam . . . banana jam . . . trifle jam . . . bleurgh, soap water jam,' (this was just soap water in the sink, but it didn't dampen Horace's enthusiasm). 'This place is amazing!' exclaimed Horace, now covered head to toe in a multi-coloured mat of jam.

Horace's mind had been blown. The young food connoisseur could not control himself. 'I'm just going to grab about a thousand scones from Mrs Barber's grocery shop', he said. 'I'll be back in a jiffy!'

Horace was gone in a flash. You could almost see a Horace-shaped cloud of dust where he had been standing.

Sam walked over to Grandad who had ignored Horace's excitement altogether and stared pensively into the fire.

'Grandad, are you okay?'

The flames trembled in his eyes.

'I need to show you something, Sam.'

CHAPTER

8

S am and Grandad walked a short distance to the nearby cliff, then down a steep set of steps to the small harbour where Grandad's wooden boat was tied up.

The sea was choppy. Very choppy, in fact. But Sam trusted Grandad completely. She hopped down from the pier into the wooden boat, and Myrtle and Grandad followed.

'Where are we going?' Sam asked Grandad as they pushed off, but the old man was clearly in a world of his own and didn't answer.

Grandad rowed patiently against the waves which became larger and rougher as they left the harbour. Neither wore life jackets, such was the style at the time.

The waves splashed against the bow of the boat and soon all three were drenched. They did not speak a word. For one, it was too noisy, what with the waves smashing against the boat and the wind whistling in their ears, but Sam also knew that Grandad needed to focus on the task at hand which was somewhat treacherous.

Eventually they were far enough away from the cliff face that, when Sam looked back, she could see their warm and worn lighthouse perched at the top. Sam stared up longingly as one particularly wet wave splashed her neck and dribbled horribly down her back.

'Grandad, what are we doing here?' asked a frozen and impatient Sam. 'How much further?'

Grandad's cardigan was sodden. For several moments, he said nothing. The boat rounded a huge chunk of rock resting long and upright. It was dark and jagged and Sam imagined that it had once formed part of the cliff.

They were now facing towards the tall cliff face and the lighthouse above looked tiny by comparison. Grandad stopped rowing and flung a heavy anchor deep into the waters. The anchor plunged and the chain rattled against the boat before it came to a halt.

The evening light was fading, and the waves swished

and swirled around them. Seagulls swooped at them from above, probably thinking that they were fishermen, but Myrtle flashed her choppers which quickly frightened them off.

'What are we doing here, Grandad?' demanded a shivering Sam once more, but Grandad's attention was fixed at a point on the cliff in front of them.

She followed his gaze until she spotted the subject of his interest: a small, dark cave right at the bottom of the cliff.

'I haven't been fully honest with you, Sam,' replied Grandad, finally. 'I have to tell you a story, a true story that took place here many, many years ago.'

Sam shifted on the wooden bench to get comfortable, but that was futile in her drenched state. Myrtle rubbed her head against Sam, as if to say, *Sit up and listen.*

'Did you know I had a brother, Sam?' asked Grandad. 'No.'

'Edgar was his name. I was the older of the two. We fought, as brothers do, but he was my very best friend.'

Sam remembered the old photograph on the chest of drawers in her bedroom.

Grandad stared straight into the cave, almost looking out for something.

'We came here all the time,' he turned to look back at Sam. 'On this very boat actually . . . They don't build them like this any more.'

He patted the sturdy wood fondly.

'We had goats back then too,' said Grandad, nodding at Myrtle with a fleeting smile. 'Anyway, Edgar and I would have great adventures out here. We came to this cave very often. That was, until . . . ' Grandad's voice cracked and he looked down at his weathered hands which shook slightly.

'One day, we came out here on a summer's evening, as we often did that time of year after school. We had been fishing and had got a few bites but had caught nothing all evening. It was getting late, but it was still very blue and bright. We had already missed dinner, but Edgar pleaded, "Just a few more minutes, Jacob." In truth, I did not take too much convincing.

'The tide was out and a lot more rocks were on view. Edgar wanted to go inside the cave to the rock pools. There are crabs in the rock pools.'

Grandad sniffed and Sam was unsure if he was teary

eyed or getting a cold, perhaps both equally likely in the circumstances.

He paused before continuing, 'I told him . . . I told him, "No, Edgar, we must go home." He didn't listen to me. He jumped into the water and hopped up onto the rocks before entering into the cave. At that time, the wind began to howl and the weather suddenly darkened. I was overcome with fear. I shouted after Edgar, "Come back!" But he did not respond – it was as if he couldn't hear me. The wind howled louder and, curiously, it seemed that the louder I called, the louder the wind whistled, until . . . '

'Until what?' asked Sam.

'There was something in there, Sam,' continued Grandad. 'It was not man or woman, nor dog, nor goat. It was not even solid, but I saw something *ghostly* and when I called Edgar again, there was no reply.'

'Was he okay?' pressed Sam, who had momentarily forgotten that she was soaked from head to toe.

'Well, at first I thought he was joking, hiding – he had that sense of humour. But he did not reappear . . . Then I began to fear the worst. I thought he was gone, in truth. I stayed anchored out all night long in the dark;

I could not return home without Edgar. At sunrise, I was about to give up, but suddenly he emerged.'

'What? He spent all night in the cave? You must have been so relieved to see him!'

'Well, I was overjoyed,' he replied. 'Of course, I was. I'd feared the worst, yet here he was, my brother in the flesh. But almost instantly, I knew it was not him. It looked like him, sure it did. He wore the same clothes, he had the same dark hair, he spoke in the same voice, but he was not himself.'

The evening sky was getting darker, and Myrtle leaned forward, nudging Grandad from his almost trance-like state. Grandad came to and patted Myrtle in thanks. He turned back around and faced Sam.

'From that moment on, we were not so close,' continued Grandad. 'In fact, we barely spoke at all. He was more stranger than brother. There was an emptiness about him. A soullessness.

'Edgar and I both left home at a very young age, it was more common back then. He took his path, I took mine. I went on my travels and met your grandmother, and we soon had your mother. Eventually we returned to Draymur Isle and settled down in our lighthouse.

'I've kept to myself for many years now, ever since your grandmother died. In truth, I have not seen my Edgar for a long time.'

The sea was getting rougher and the wind howled.

'You can say what you like, Sam, that this is life and people drift apart, but someone does not change so abruptly like that without intervention. It was a silentrap that possessed him that day. I know it in my gut. And you must always trust your gut, Sam.'

Grandad was very convincing, and Sam cared deeply for him, but she could not be certain of anything he said. This all sounded insane. Her brain was reluctant, but her heart told her to listen.

As Sam watched Grandad look longingly into the dark cavern, she felt a pang deep inside. Although his was different, she felt his loss. In a way, talk of monsters was a very welcome distraction from her parents' passing. She felt that nothing could match the pain she was feeling inside.

'I bet you miss him a lot,' said Sam, and all of a sudden she was very glad to be soaked by the sea so that Grandad could not tell she was crying.

Grandad took Sam's hand and looked her straight in the eyes.

'You cannot trust this island, Sam. Never, ever go inside that cave, do you understand me?'

Sam nodded in silence and Grandad wiped away her tears.

No more was said. Together they lifted the heavy anchor and they made their way back to the lighthouse without another word.

* * *

It was nearly dark when they arrived back. Horace sat waiting with two very large black sacks.

'Where have you been?' he asked, half a scone in his mouth. 'You're soaked.'

Sam looked back at Grandad who said nothing. They were both exhausted.

'We had to secure the boat,' lied Sam. 'Stormy waters.'

This excuse seemed to satisfy Horace who was keen to get inside the jam-filled lighthouse.

As soon as they entered, Grandad attended to the fading fire, while Horace spilled the contents of one of the black sacks onto the small table. Dozens of scones cascaded from the big bag onto the jammy table, many onto the jammy floor.

'There must be around two hundred scones here, Horace,' exclaimed Sam.

'Mrs Barber gave me twice the number I asked for,' said Horace with a grin. 'Very decent of her. I had to let her cut my hair, though.'

Mrs Barber was not a talented hairdresser. Judging by Horace's haircut, Sam felt the lady might be more suited to work as the village butcher.

A fringeless Horace picked up a scone and dipped it into the coal bucket (which, if you remember, was full of black coal jam, not dark chocolate jam as he believed).

'So,' said Horace, his lips now covered in the dark jam, 'remind me why you have jam smeared all over the place again.'

'Are you sure you want to know?' asked Sam.

'*Of coff, of coff,*' replied Horace, his mouth stuffed, 'of course.' He swallowed, then took a large handful of coal jam.

Truth be told, Sam was unsure about Grandad's stories. But he was all she had, and she had to be loyal to him.

She inhaled deeply before speaking, aware of how bizarre this next sentence might sound.

'The jam is to keep the splochers away, Horace,' she said plainly.

Horace froze in his stride, his mouth *full* of jam. Not just that, but his hands and face were covered in jam. Not just *that*, but his hair and jumper were caked in jam. Not just *that* – oh, I think you get the idea. Horace looked a right mess.

'Splochers, ah yes, you mentioned those before, Sam,' he said calmly, before rising to his feet and wiping his chin clean. 'Right, well, it's been lovely seeing you all. Thank you for your hospitality, but I best be off.'

He began to walk a quick and squelchy walk to the door.

SQUICK-SQUElCH-SQUICK-SQUElCH-SQUICK-SQUElCH!

'Do enjoy the scones,' he said, waving hurriedly. 'Very nice with jam apparently.'

But before he could make it over to the door, there came a growl.

Myrtle.

The goat had a glint in her eye.

80

Chapter 8

Horace looked at the goat, then the door. The goat, the door . . . the door, the goat.

'I wouldn't run,' warned Grandad. 'You need to hear this, Hatchet. Your father's denial about these monsters won't help you.'

Horace sat down by the fire, Myrtle's watchful eyes sticking to him like jam.

'All right, all right,' sighed Horace. 'My dad spoke to me once about monsters under the bed. He said that . . .'

'Said *what?*' asked Grandad gruffly.

Horace grimaced (perhaps from the bitter aftertaste of coal jam). 'He said that you made it up years ago to scare children in your class and that you were eventually expelled because you were a complete loon and wouldn't stop harassing everyone on the island about your weird theories.'

Grandad let these words sink in, smacking Horace's hand away from a defenceless scone.

'Weird theories,' said Grandad, placing both hands on his walking stick as if contemplating.

'I'm sorry, sir,' said Horace, nibbling at a top-secret scone from up his sleeve. 'It's just what he said.'

The fire began to *snap*, *crackle* and *pop* like a rather well-known breakfast cereal.

'Horace,' said Sam, taking a leap of faith in her grandfather. 'Your father has it all wrong.'

Sam told him about the splochers that munch and crunch a child's feet and hands. She told him about the serpentails that wringle and wrangle before draining a child dry like a refreshing glass of prune juice. She even told him about the silentraps, how they camouflage their sound and take over a child's body. She paused only to allow for Horace's occasional whimpers.

But she did not tell him about Edgar. That was Grandad's and her secret.

Needless, to say, Horace was appropriately petrified.

'Are you sure about all this, Sam?' asked Horace nervously.

'Positive,' replied Sam, although she was far from it. 'And I'm going to prove it to you.'

CHAPTER
9

Usually Horace loved a good old-fashioned sleepover. On this occasion, however, he was not at all excited and had to be bribed with fizzy cola jam that tanged treacherously on his tongue. Myrtle too was very persuasive, snarling aggressively by the front door which was the main point of exit.

'Remember what I told you,' warned Grandad from his trusted armchair. 'Jam on your toes and feet and fingers and hands and–'

'Yes, Grandad, I know.'

'And remember, Sam,' said Grandad. 'If any serpentails get you, laugh!'

Sam smiled, slightly unconvinced by all of Grandad's warnings. 'Yes, Grandad.'

Horace watched the back and forth like a spectator at a particularly gripping tennis match.

'And don't forget to use the nicknames in case any silentraps make an appearance,' finished Grandad.

Grandad had given Horace the nickname *Jammy Sod*, a nod perhaps towards Horace's love of jam but also Grandad's dislike of Horace and his family.

'Yes, Grandad.'

Grandad smiled at Sam.

'Hatchet,' he said gruffly.

'Yes?' asked Horace nervously.

'Hands and feet where I can see them!'

With some difficulty, Sam and Horace had shifted a spare bed up to Sam's circular bedroom. It was dusty, and creaky, and smelly, but it had four legs and stood a safe distance off the ground.

Horace sat on his bed and opened a jar of spaghetti bolognese jam. He quickly began to lather it all over his hands and feet. Sam sat on her own bed thoughtfully.

'Aren't you going to put jam on like your grandad said?' asked Horace.

'Well,' considered Sam. 'If I am going to prove that

splochers exists, I had better leave off the jam to attract them, hadn't I?'

'Isn't that dangerous?'

'So, you believe in these monsters under the bed then?'

'No . . . no, of course not,' replied Horace unconvincingly, scrubbing the jam onto his head and shoulders.

As always on the island, the wind howled all around, but even more so in the lighthouse because of its location right next to the cliff edge. The two lay back on their beds listening to it and to the waves crashing outside.

'It's quite noisy in here,' said Horace. 'Don't you find it hard to sleep?'

'I find it quite relaxing, actually,' said Sam.

And so, after a major sugar crash, Horace drifted off. Soon, Sam too began to snore like a piglet.

BANG–BANG–BANG!

Sam and Horace both bolted upright in their beds. For a moment they sat utterly confused, half-asleep. Then instinctively, they both looked down at the floor, but there was not a splocher nor a serpentail in sight.

Then it came again. Even louder this time.

BANG–BANG–BANG!

Rather incredibly, right outside Sam's window, which you'll remember made up the entire bedroom wall, stood Ivy and Wesley, perched perilously on a ladder. They were dressed in old ragged white sheets and wore white face paint. They mocked Sam and Horace loudly as they slammed the glass with the palms of their hands.

'WooooOOOOOOOOOOOOOOOOOOOOOOOO!'
wailed Ivy cruelly.

Wesley stood alongside his sister, laughing, before he chimed in loudly, 'Saaaaaaaam! Horaaaaace! We are the monsters under the beeeeed! We have come to eat yooooou!'

The twins found this all quite hysterical. Although Sam was angry, she could not help but admire their sheer fearlessness: standing high atop the lighthouse on the side of a stormy cliff, just to give them a scare. Life on the island was clearly dull if this was their idea of fun.

Sam and Horace got out of their beds and walked over to the glass. Ivy and Wesley stood on the other side just a few feet away. Wesley clasped his mouth to the glass and made very rude noises against the window while Ivy wailed again. The two of them broke into uncontrollable laughter.

The twins were laughing so hard that they were on the verge of passing out. They paused for breath which was a mistake. A big mistake. For what came next cannot *stand* a child's laughter.

SMASH!

For a moment, Sam could not believe what she was seeing. After all, it was still dark and the only light came from the moon and the night sky which was a dull grey colour. All she could hear was Ivy's high-pitched screaming. Sam's eyes adapted to the gloom and her jaw dropped.

Wesley was held high over the cliff, being dangled by his ankle. At first, Sam thought he was being clasped by a great snake and for a split second, although she

would never say it aloud, she was overjoyed to see the shock on Wesley's face and the fear in Ivy's eyes.

But then she realised what was before her.

Her jaw dropped.

A serpentail.

A slimy black tentacle was stretched from under Sam's bed, right past her and Horace, and out the window, where it clenched Wesley tightly. It was covered in large suckers like an octopus. Before Sam could react, two, then three, then four more of these skinny snake-like arms flew out from under her bed. Within seconds, Wesley's arms and legs were wrapped by the serpentails, who were swinging him from side to side like a rag doll.

Wesley screamed in terror.

Sam snapped into action.

'Wesley!' yelled Sam, but the boy was, understandably, rather distracted.

'Heeeeeeeeeeeeeeeeeeeeelp'–he yelled as he was being swung from one side to the other–'meeeeeeeeeee!'

Wesley's movement reminded Sam of a theme park she had been to some years earlier with her parents. Although the danger was obvious, the tiniest part of Sam smirked as she imagined a funfair featuring serpentail swings that swung Wesley around and around until he threw up.

'Do something!' shouted Ivy.

'Wesley!' shouted Sam, remembering Grandad's advice. 'You've got to laugh. I know it sounds crazy, but you have to try!'

Within seconds, Wesley was wrapped up by *at least* ten serpentails, and it was hard to see him.

Now Sam began to panic. She tried to think of something funny. But comedy is all about timing, and it felt like the wrong time to tell a joke.

As she was wracking her brains thinking of knock-knock jokes, she heard another unwelcome sound behind her.

SHHHCLUMP!

Sam stood perfectly still. Her sweat ran cold.

Before she could consider the noise further, it came again. Except this time, it was louder, clumsier.

SSSHHHHCLUMP–UMP– UMP!

Chapter 9

Then came gurgling, gargling sounds.

Veeery slowly, she turned. What faced her was quite possibly more terrifying than the serpentails stretching into the air, trying to drain Wesley like a refreshing glass of prune juice.

Like legless, snot-covered hyenas, two beasts snarled and sniped. They growled viciously and through the dim light, Sam could see the red dots that were unmistakably their cruel eyes. She could also make out a terrifying collection of yellow spiked teeth. She could hear their bellies rumble, readying themselves for a gassy stinking attack.

The smaller splocher shimmied forward first, its belly squeaking and scrunching awkwardly across the floorboards.

Then came the sound of curiosity.

SNIFF-SNIFF-SNIFF . . .

SNIFF-SNIFF-SNIFF . . .

SNIFF-SNIFF-SNIIIIIIIIIIFF!

'Shis a new crimmpler,' said the smaller of the splochers. Its voice was wispy and high pitched. Whiny and unsettling. 'I is wants to *tashte* that *juicy* crimmpler.'

Sam could hear the splochers' bellies gurgle and gargle. She could tell they were not going to hold back much longer. At any moment, they would blast from their rear ends and fly through the air at her.

'Shis a specials crimmpler,' slurped the larger of the two, a menacing smile across its ugly face. 'Mortempra will be overjoyist. But she won'ts minds if I avs justs a little shnopster. Just a toes or a toe tack. Or an eyes or an ears or a sneezer.'

The splocher slurped grotesquely, shimmied forward and, of course you will remember, Reader, that Sam was not wearing any protective jam, so she really was the perfect snack. In fact, she was the most delicious, defenceless-looking crimmpler a splocher could ever ask for.

Yes, the situation was desperate.

Wesley was wrapped up high in the air by the serpentails.

Ivy was screaming loudly, which made it very difficult to concentrate.

And Sam looked as though she would also become the victim of a scrumptious crime.

Worse still, but *more* splochers could be heard

shimmying out from under the bed – at least three more and counting – and Sam could make out their viciously wonky outlines. Some splochers stopped to gobble up some stray socks and Sam suddenly realized where her shoes had disappeared to.

The growing number of splochers steadily advanced towards Sam.

SSSHHHHCLUMP–UMP– UMP–UMP . . .

But, this would be a very tragic and unsatisfying ending to this story and, quite frankly, Reader, I prefer something a bit more upbeat . . . more triumphant . . .

And so, there came a slicing sound. Loud, yet clean.

SWISH through the air it sounded, then *THUD!*

Then it came again, louder this time.

SWISH through the air, and *THUD!*

AND AGAIN!

Sam clasped her eyes shut and covered her ears as the slicing continued.

Then suddenly there was nothing.

No growling or grumbling.

No gripping or hissing.

When Sam opened her eyes, Wesley lay on her bedroom floor wrapped up in serpentail remains, like a full, undrunk glass of prune juice.

The vine-like snakes from under the bed had been sliced to pieces. The splochers too were a gooey mess.

Ivy climbed carefully through the widow and rushed to Wesley's aid, unravelling the serpentail remains from his arms and legs. Ivy and Sam helped Wesley sit up and looked up across the room.

To their surprise, there stood Horace Hatchet with a sharp, now rather slimy-looking, hatchet that glistened in the moonlight.

Chapter 9

Sam smiled at her friend.

While Horace hated the idea of butchering animals, he clearly had no problem whatsoever protecting his classmates, even those who probably didn't deserve it. And I must say, Reader, despite his awful haircut, he looked very pleased with himself indeed.

CHAPTER
10

Within seconds, Grandad and Myrtle barged in through the door.

Sam, Horace and Ivy began to speak all at once, while Wesley sat sheepishly on the floor.

'One at a time,' said Grandad. 'One at a time, I said!'

'Serpentails, then splochers,' began Sam, flustered. 'They all . . . there were lots of them . . . they could have killed us . . . if it weren't for Horace . . . '

Grandad ushered the group downstairs to the kitchen, with Myrtle bringing up the rear, and poured them all a cup of jam tea.

Sam took a sip. It was sweet, of course, and rather sludgy, as you can imagine, but it was comforting and gave her the composure she needed. She explained everything that had happened.

'Couldn't you hear anything, Grandad?' she asked quietly. It occurred to her that he had not come running immediately, even with all their screaming.

'Honestly, Sam, I had no idea. I didn't hear a thing. But that must mean . . . Oh, no.'

'What, Grandad?'

'That a silentrap was in the room with you tonight. I know I told you that they steal the sound of your screams, but I do wonder why they would turn up to a run-of-the-mill splocher attack . . .'

'They were talking about something or someone called Mortempra. Have you heard that name before, Grandad?'

Grandad shook his head. He looked worried.

'I can't say I have.'

No one said anything while Grandad thought deeply. Finally, he spoke.

'Serves you right, you two,' he snapped, turning to face the Gardiner twins. 'Sneaking around in the middle of the night like that. I should tell your parents!'

'Please don't,' cried Ivy, standing, her head bowed in apology. 'We're really sorry.'

'Yeah, we're really sorry,' added Wesley, massaging his neck which was bruised red. 'And for the damage to your windows – we'll fix them.'

'And Hatchet!' added Grandad. 'I had you all wrong. Good lad.'

Horace's eyes twinkled at the praise.

'Grandad, we've got to do something!' Sam chimed in. 'Those monsters under the bed nearly ate us for a midnight feast. If we don't do something they could eat every child on the island, and who knows what else.'

'You're right,' said Grandad, pacing from side to side, his cane squidging into the jam at every third step. Myrtle followed in his footsteps faithfully, so their shoes and hooves squished and squelched as they paced.

'These attacks . . . ' he muttered, almost to himself. 'They're so open – they don't seem to be bothering to hide.'

The shoes and hooves continued to squish and squelch for a while, but no one spoke.

'Well,' said Sam thoughtfully, breaking the silence. 'What if we were to hunt them like they hunt us?'

'Hunt them?' asked Ivy. 'Like, to *eat*? I am NOT eating

those splochit thingies or serpentallies or whatever you call them.'

'*Splochers* and *serpentails*,' corrected Grandad, wondering what had happened to the schooling system on Draymur Isle.

'Could you imagine the stomach-ache after eating a splocher?' said Horace, a look of horror on his face. 'You'd be glued to the toilet for days . . . '

'No, what I mean is, we need to stand up for ourselves,' said Sam. 'We need to show them that we're not afraid and that we will protect ourselves. We need to fight back!'

'Sam's right,' agreed Hatchet. 'Look, I'm a Hatchet!'

'The boy's gone mad,' muttered Grandad.

'No, as in, I'm a Hatchet and all Hatchets are butchers,' said Horace.

'I thought you didn't like butchering animals,' said Wesley.

'Not defenceless animals. But creatures that want to get children? I've no problem chopping them up,' smiled Horace. 'And there are weapons everywhere we look. I have a hatchet, for one. And there are fire pokers, and knives . . . and sheets of paper.'

'Paper?' asked Wesley.

'Have you ever had a papercut?' replied Horace. 'Nasty little things.'

'I'm not so sure about this,' said Wesley.

'Me neither,' added Ivy.

'What do you mean?' demanded Sam. 'You were fine to climb up the lighthouse and slam on my bedroom window a few minutes ago. Where's your courage now?'

'It's not us,' said Wesley. 'Our parents will be really mad if they hear about any of this.'

'But these monsters are real, and they will eat us!' urged Sam. 'They won't stop!'

The room fell silent.

'I've seen them before,' said Horace, finally opening up. 'Splochers. I've hid from them, but they were there, under the bed. When I told my father he went nuts. He said I was making it all up. Eventually I started to doubt if I'd even seen them.'

'The people on this island,' said Grandad. 'They live in denial. They live in fear.'

Sam turned to Ivy and Wesley. 'Are you both telling me that you have *never* seen a splocher or a serpentail?'

The twins glanced at one another, before reluctantly answering.

'Fine,' conceded Ivy. 'I may have seen one of those snakes once.'

'Yeah,' agreed Wesley. 'Maybe once. Or twice.'

Sam considered the twins. They were so scared of their parents that they would not fight for the truth, even it meant having their toes bitten off, or being drunk dry. Or worse!

'That's it,' said Sam. 'This ends now. First thing tomorrow, we rally the classroom – let everyone know our plan! It's us or the monsters! Let's turn the hunters into the *hunted*!'

Sam raised a glass of jam tea to toast.

Grandad, Myrtle, and Horace stared at the Gardiner twins.

Ivy and Wesley looked at one another, then smiled and nodded.

CLINK!

The plan was set.

CHAPTER
11

Bright and early the next morning, Sam, Horace, Ivy, and Wesley walked through the school gates. There were very few children in the school and their class was small, only ten pupils, so it did not take long for them all to gather behind the old shed, well out of sight of Major Chase.

Besides Sam, Horace, Ivy, and Wesley, there was:

Sally Baker, the baker's daughter, a supremely talented baker and an even more gifted yodeller. Every morning she was up at the crack of dawn baking and yodelling loudly (having replaced the island rooster some years earlier). She was known across Draymur Isle for her delicious

Chapter 11

Yodel Strudel. She had blonde hair, rosy cheeks and a wicked laugh.

Tom Cheeseman, the cheesemonger's son, who had an unhealthy addiction to cheese. A *chain cheeser*, as he was known, he was never without a large block of cheddar cheese. He was surprisingly thin with brown hair and a wicked smell.

Billy Fisher, the fishmonger's son, a big lad who always carried a fishing rod and had an even wickeder smell than Cheeseman. He had a fiercely accurate aim with his rod. He could catch almost anything, most often the common cold as he fished without the proper attire.

Audrey Shepard, the shepherd's daughter, was a red-haired girl who always had a sheep or two with her. She wore sheep wool every day of the year and was often itchy and irritable (which was particularly trying for her classmates during the summer months). She prided herself at having the loudest and most piercing whistle this side of the moon.

Henry Slater, the roofer's son, a gangly boy who enjoyed climbing on top of anything: a house, a tree, a human pyramid when his classmates were willing (usually on his birthday).

Last, and nearly always late, Walt Weaver, whose father was the island's weaver, and mother, the island's insurance salesperson. A shy boy with an inability to be on time for anything (class, appointments, and even his own birth – famously arriving three months late). He had been the victim of nearly all of Major Chase's homemade dentistry treatments, which included tongue scraping (with a garden rake), molar sanding (with an electric sander from Major Chase's boot) and cleaning (which involved his two front teeth actually being sent to the mainland for dry cleaning). Weaver was the smallest in the class which made his helmet of braces look even more enormous.

'We don't have much time, you lot,' called Ivy. 'Listen up, Sam has something important to tell you.'

Sam sensed that Ivy and Wesley had control of the playground, and Ivy had control over Wesley, so it was probably best to keep her onside.

The pupils gathered around to hear Sam out.

Baker was first to pipe up, yodelling loudly at Sam (enjoy reading this next bit aloud, Reader).

'YoU're the nE-Ew giiiirl,' she sang, her voice wobbling rapidly and repeatedly. 'You live in the ligh-IGHt-hOOOUse!'

'Shush, Baker!' said Wesley, grimacing and holding his ears.

'Eh, yeah, that's right,' said Sam, who had forgotten that she had yet to win over the rest of the class.

'Why are your feet so big?' asked Cheeseman, his voice heavy with suspicion. He was gnawing on a huge chunk of particularly mature red cheddar (it was only the strong stuff for Cheeseman).

Sam had yet to replace her shoes that were stolen by the splocher the other night, so she had been forced to wear Grandad's fishing boots again.

'Shut it, Cheesy!' said Wesley menacingly.

Everyone clamped shut.

'Right, well, em,' started Sam. 'I'm sure you may have heard of them before but . . . em, I don't know how to say this . . .'

'Monsters under the bed are real!' blurted Horace. 'You know it, I know it, we all know it, so let's stop living in denial!'

The whole class gasped.

'Is this some weird– ah-ahhhh-CHOO!' said Fisher. He had caught a fresh cold earlier that morning. 'Is this some weird joke? Because it's not funny . . . Not that they're real, of course.'

'They are real!' cried Sam. 'We saw them last night.'

Ivy and Wesley began to describe the events of the previous evening.

'This is all a load of sheep poo,' interrupted Shepard irritably. She scratched and scratched and scratched as she continued. 'What's the angle here? Whenever the Gardiner twins are involved, there's an angle.'

'Listen, everyone,' began Slater. 'I've been working on a new human pyramid technique. I think I figured out the problem from the last time. You see, the person on top should go on *last*.'

'Not now, Slater!' spiked Ivy.

The class broke into a row. In fact, it went on for some time. This book could have contained page after page of irrelevant dialogue.

SSSHHLAAAP!

There was a sudden silence as the class looked around in shock. There before them lay a gruesome lifeless splocher.

'Here's the proof,' said Horace. '*This* tried to eat us last night.'

There was an unidentifiable whimper from the crowd (although my money is on Fisher).

The splocher's mouth hung open wide like a shark and its countless killer teeth were clear for all to see.

'What is that?' asked Baker, looking as pale as a bag of flour.

'You've seen it before,' said Horace. 'I know you all have.'

'It's a splocher,' said Sam.

'And this – give me a hand, Wesley' – continued Horace – 'is a serpentail.'

The two boys heaved the serpentail out of Horace's bag; not that it was heavy, but it was quite bulky and difficult to hold. It was long, and black, and sticky, although its suckers were dark grey.

The class stared at the grotesque-looking monsters. All that could be heard was a rusty swing as it moved back and forward in the distance, slowly and eerily (very original, I know).

'I've seen one of those before,' said Weaver eventually, pointing at the splocher.

He looked Sam in the eyes.

'I've seen them quite a few times,' he continued. 'One nearly ate me a few months ago. I haven't been able to sleep at night since. That's why I'm always late – I always drift off when the sun rises. They never come after the sun rises.'

There was a moment's silence as the class let this sink in.

'Last Christmas,' said Fisher suddenly, 'one of those snake things clasped itself around my arm while I was sleeping.'

Chapter 11

'How did you get it off?' asked Sam.

'It was in the middle of a blackout and our electricity was off, so I had a candle next to my bed,' explained Fisher. 'I grabbed it and held the flame against its suckers – I guess that scared it away. Now I always keep a candle next to my bed just in case.'

Sam took this on board: *The serpentails don't like fire as well as children's laughter.*

One by one, each of their classmates stood forward, each revealing their various brushes with these monsters.

One of Cheeseman's dangling hands had been nipped by a young splocher: 'A bigger one would have taken the whole hand,' he said. 'This is why I always wear rubber gloves – to hide the scars from all of you.'

His classmates had always thought it was to do with health and safety. After all, his family sold cheese to everyone on the island.

Baker was next and spoke in her non-yodel voice, which was surprisingly steady: 'A serpentail sucked so much blood from my foot that my leg shrivelled up like a prune for a month.'

Sam wondered what it was about these islanders and their prunes, but she kept quiet.

Slater had a big toe nabbed by a splocher when he was eight, which probably explained why he kept causing the collapse of human pyramids.

Shepard frequently had her sheep wool stolen by these creatures. 'The greedy pests,' she muttered resentfully.

On and on and on, the various attacks came out, until finally, almost everyone had said their bit.

'Eh, the splochers eat my homework every night,' lied Wesley opportunistically.

'Your parents didn't believe any of you, did they?' asked Sam.

'How did you know?' asked Weaver.

'Because only children can see the markings left by a splocher,' she explained. 'Or the marks left by any of these creatures for that matter.'

'Every time I told my parents, they got really annoyed,' explained Weaver. 'To punish me, they made me eat dessert for dinner, which completely put me off my dessert. And I love dessert!'

Next, Slater piped up.

'My parents accused me of lying. They made me wear a tongue corrector for weeks so I would stop telling lies. I couldn't eat anything but milk soup. Milk soup!

That's just warm milk! Do you know how constipated I was?'

'Didn't you drink any prune juice?' asked Horace, with nodding approval from his classmates.

'Well, this can't happen any more,' said Sam determinedly. 'We have ways to fight back.'

She told them all about Horace and his hatchet, and how brilliant he had been. She told them that splochers *hate* jam; that, as well as being afraid of fire, serpentails *despise* the sound of children's laughter; and that silentraps can possess a child's body (as if Weaver needed another reason not to sleep at night).

'These monsters are dangerous, and we've got to do something about them,' she continued. 'So arm yourself at night – with jam, of course, *and* laughter . . . and fire, and nicknames too – everyone must have a nickname so we can tell if a silentrap has possessed you. Remember they're great at impersonations!'

'How can we kill them though?' asked Fisher.

'Use your imagination,' urged Sam.

'I used my trusted hatchet,' said Horace proudly.

'I could weave a web to trap them,' said Weaver eagerly.

'I could catch them with my fishing net!' exclaimed Fisher.

'I suppose I could use a few wheels of warm Camembert cheese,' said Cheeseman, as if making the ultimate sacrifice. 'Those serpentails won't like getting stuck in that stuff.'

'I could crush them with some roof slates,' said Slater.

'Or big bags of flour,' Baker added.

'Brilliant, everyone,' said Sam excitedly. 'And remember, whatever you do, stay in bed.'

'But what if I need to go to the toilet?' asked Shepard.

'Hold it in,' said Sam. 'The hunters shall become the hunted!'

The class nattered excitedly; the plan was set. And just in time too, as the school bell chimed and they bolted inside to Major Chase and his hungry pliers.

CHAPTER
12

The next day was Saturday (my favourite day after bin day).

Sam's class had arranged to meet at the lighthouse for their first progress report. They had decided to meet late, after their parents had all gone to bed and to avoid any awkward questions. But they were careful to wear jam, and to laugh a lot, and to use nicknames to avoid splochers, and serpentails, and (as best they could) silentraps.

Given the nature of the meeting, Grandad had no issue whatsoever with their gatherings taking place in his house: 'Reminds me of the olden days,' he said as he tossed a piece of wood into the fire.

He had again smeared jam onto his face. Not that he

needed to (because, as an elderly man, he would taste like burnt toast to a splocher) but he liked to be involved.

'How so, Grandad?' asked Sam.

'It brings it all back,' replied Grandad, now rubbing jam onto Myrtle's face, making her look like a real warrior. 'Fighting splochers and serpentails always made me feel alive.'

There came a cautious knock at the door.

Sam squished and squelched her way through the jam to open it.

'Nickname?' she called.

'*Jammy Sod*,' replied Horace.

Sam opened the door to find most of her classmates huddled together like penguins. It was dark out and the rain was whipping left, right and centre, so the small lighthouse was a warm and cosy refuge. The classmates quickly announced their passwords and bundled inside. You don't need to know all the nicknames, Reader. Suffice to say, they were all sharp and witty, each as chucklesome as the last. (And besides, if I had to go through each one, they'd catch their death out there.)

By this stage, Horace, Ivy and Wesley were well used to the sounds and smells of jam inside the lighthouse,

Chapter 12

but it took the others a moment to get used to it. They grinned at the different types of jam dripping from the ceiling and the walls and glooping on the floor and the furniture.

The room was filled with light thanks to the blazing fire and the hundred or so candles Grandad had lit 'to keep serpentails away and toe-stubbing at bay'. The sheer volume of jam was mesmerizing: it sparkled in the candlelight and glistened like treasure.

'Come on in,' said Sam. 'Grab a seat wherever you can.'

Cheeseman immediately went for the cheese board on the kitchen table (addiction is a terrible thing) which was, of course, completely covered in jam. 'Is that' – he took a taste – 'cheddar cheese jam?'

'I don't know,' replied Sam.

'That's definitely blue cheese jam!' he exclaimed, nodding approvingly, and dipping a finger into a bluey, cheesy blob.

'Where's Weaver?' asked Sam.

''ee is aways la'e,' said Fisher, his mouth already full of pickled herring jam.

With that, there came a worried-sounding knock at

the door. How could a knock sound worried, you ask? Well, Weaver had a knack. And a knock.

The nervous boy fell in through the door, out of breath and drenched to the skin.

'Sorry . . . I'm . . . late,' he breathed heavily, taking a hit of his asthma inhaler through his helmet of braces.

'Password, Weaver?' Sam reminded him.

'Oh, sorry – *I hate Major Chase.*'

Weaver dragged a massive suitcase in through the doorway.

It was then that Sam realized that they *all* had a huge array of packed bags.

Weaver even had bags under his eyes.

'What's in the bags?' asked Sam, predictably.

For a moment there was no reply. The classmates all looked at one another grinning, then Weaver, the now-not-so-shy boy, stepped forward.

'Well, after our meeting we were inspired,' he said.

'Yeah,' continued Shepard. 'We decided we were fed up of these creatures chomping our toes, and sucking our blood, and taking our wool.'

'And our homework!' added Wesley.

Chapter 12

'We each took it upon ourselves to, well, do as you said,' said Fisher. 'And more–'

'So,' interrupted Ivy, 'we went home like you said and armed ourselves with jam, and jokes, and nicknames, and a few tricks that we came up with ourselves, and . . .'

'And what?' asked Sam excitedly.

Weaver weaved between his classmates to his suitcase and *ZzzzZZIP!* opened it to reveal the largest splocher Grandad had ever seen.

'That's the largest splocher I have ever seen!' said Grandad, confirming the previous sentence.

The splocher's face was ugly and cruel and lifeless. Its teeth were sharp and plentiful. It was green and looked like a cross between an angry frog and a mild-mannered crocodile.

'But how did you do it, Weaver?' asked Sam, thrilled but stunned.

Weaver stood straight with pride, beaming from ear to ear. 'I wove a trap with my loom – a bit like a spider's web,' he explained. 'I carefully built it at the end of my bed. Then, to attract the splocher, I lay with my feet sticking out the end, with no jam on them, and, boy, did it work! Then, when it got tangled, I whacked it on the head with one of my mum's huge books on life insurance. Actually, I wonder did that splocher have life insurance . . . '

'The size of it!' exclaimed Horace, lifting the splocher with great difficulty. 'It's as heavy as a small stove!'

'Nice work, Weaver,' Wesley said, clapping.

'How about the rest of you?' asked Sam, grinning from ear to ear.

One by one, her friends explained how they got the better of their predator.

'I used my little sister as bait,' began Fisher.

Everyone in the room stared at him.

'All right, all right,' he corrected. 'I used my little sister's dolls as bait.'

Still, everyone in the room stared silently at him.

'All right, all right,' he admitted finally. 'I used *my* dolls as bait. I put them on my rod and waited for the splocher to take a bite, and, well . . . ' He opened his duffel bag to produce not one, not two, but *three* splochers!

'I caught them all on the same hook!' he said proudly.

Chapter 12

They weren't as big as Weaver's splocher, but they were, all the same, very impressive. Fisher's classmates cheered and patted their friend on the back.

'Great work, Fisher,' said Sam.

Soon there was quite a party atmosphere indeed as the group compared their bludgeoning methods. Sam felt that she had been particularly successful with her clubbing technique (using one of Grandad's heavy fishing boots to bash a splocher), but she wasn't about to fall out with her new friends.

Horace stepped forward. 'I've been thinking, everyone,' he said. 'We have our weapons, but what we need is a special jam.'

'But we've got plenty of jam, Horace,' said Sam looking around at the gleaming walls and ceiling.

'Not just any jam,' he said with a smile. 'We need to make the *ultimate* jam. A jam so sticky that it will never wash off our hands and feet, so the splochers won't come near us.'

'We could make it a multi-purpose jam,' said Fisher, excitedly. 'Flammable to scare away the serpentails!'

'A flammable jam that we rub on our hands and feet that never washes off. What could possibly go wrong?'

said Shepard sarcastically. 'Why don't we just set our pants on fire while we're at it?'

Horace's enthusiasm was unstoppable, though. He dragged a massive pot near to the fireplace and began to shout orders, his chef's blood bubbling wildly. Then, in his awful singing voice, he began:

'Let's make us a jam, to keep monsters away,
A fine, sticky jam to keep our toes safe . . . '

'This isn't a musical, Horace,' snapped Ivy. 'Just make the jam!'

Chapter 12

Although Horace stopped his singing immediately, his spirits remained high.

'In with some normal, delicious dark chocolate jam for starters' – again, mistaken for coal jam – 'what next?'

'Jelly,' yelled Weaver.

'Fudge,' called Ivy.

'Caa-aa-Aa-ndyy-YY-yyyFloo-OOo-OOOOooss!' yodelled Baker.

Into the pot the ingredients went.

'Toffee,' yelled Slater.

'Bubble gum,' called Shepard.

'Sticks to make it sticky,' called Weaver.

The children sprinted around the room, finding the stickiest ingredients they could find.

'Glue,' called Sam.

'Jellybeans,' yelled Ivy.

'Marmalade,' shouted Wesley.

Horace stopped stirring abruptly. 'Marmalade? Marmalade! This is a *JAM*!' roared Horace, the fire flashing in his head chef's eyes.

'Okay, no marmalade! Forget the marmalade!' said Wesley, waving his hands defensively.

'What else?' called Horace.

'Chocolate swirls,' yelled Slater.

'Sellotape,' shouted Ivy.

'Marshmallows to make it flammable,' yelled Fisher.

'Brilliant! What else?'

On and on and on.

The jam began to gloop and bubble tremendously, as Horace stirred and stirred continuously.

'Blu-tack,' shouted Ivy.

'Chutney,' yelled Cheeseman.

'More sticks to make it even stickier,' called Weaver.

More and more and more sticky ingredients were thrown in. A pinky-purply-reddy mist wafted from the pot and the room smelled exactly like a sweet factory (which I can only imagine smells quite sticky).

'We're nearly there,' cried Horace. 'I think it just needs one final ingredient. What else?'

'Mbaaaaaaaaaaa!' yelled Myrtle, who was growing impatient.

Horace stopped stirring immediately. 'On second thoughts, you're absolutely right, Myrtle,' he said, avoiding the goat's gaze. 'No more ingredients required.'

The group stared into the pot, the warm misty goodness hitting their faces.

'What will you call it, Horace?' asked Sam.

Horace considered the question for a moment. 'How about *Horace's Ultimate Sticky Jam for Keeping Monsters Away*?'

'Mbaaaaaaaaaaaa!' Myrtle chimed in.

'I mean, how about *Myrtle's Ultimate Sticky Jam for Keeping Monsters Away*?'

The room nodded with approval while Horace sat nervously alongside Myrtle.

For now, the children felt safe and secure, feeling that they could truly beat these vile monsters.

But I'm afraid that danger waited just over the page.

CHAPTER
13

The group chatted excitedly long into the night, a
new-found confidence spreading throughout the
room.

After all, with this ultimate sticky jam coated to their
fingers, and hands, and toes, and feet, and face, and . . .
oh, I think you get the idea, Reader: they were covered
in the stuff.

Yes, they felt overwhelmingly confident as they
nattered away into the wee hours. It was late and Sam
felt it best that they all stay over, at least until the sun
rose when they could sneak home in safety. So Grandad
pulled out some old hammocks that he had made many
years ago from torn fishing nets.

'We used to use these all the time in the war,' said

Grandad, as he ensured each was tied tightly and high enough off the ground that no splochers could reach. Sam was never sure which of Grandad's stories were real and which were greatly exaggerated.

The group hopped into their sleeping nets, while Grandad and Myrtle took the armchair.

As Sam lay down, she was happy and merry and sleepy. Her eyes weighed down and she began to snore like a bulldog.

She began to dream of a day she'd spent in the park with her parents. It was raining lightly but the sun shone brightly. They ate chocolate ice cream with large chocolate flakes and chocolate sprinkles. Life did not get better than this.

'Wake up, Sam!'

Sam jolted. Her eyes snapped open.

The cosy lighthouse was upside down. No, wait, *she* was upside down – being dangled. She had no clue what was going on.

'Wake up, Sam!' yelled Grandad again.

Sam could not move.

As she peered down (or up) she saw them. Serpentails gripped her body completely. From the corner of her eyes she could see her classmates, each of them bound as tightly to their hammocks as she was; held fast by dozens and dozens of serpentails.

There was no fight. No resistance. The room was eerily quiet but for the sound of a horrible, harmonious hissing.

Sam struggled to breathe. The serpentails were grasping tighter and tighter around her chest.

'Sam!' yelled Grandad next to his armchair, now swinging at the serpentails with a fire poker. 'You've got to laugh like you mean it. Remember, the serpentails can't stand the sound of children's laughter.'

But Sam could barely breathe, let alone laugh.

Then, from across the room she saw Fisher who was mouthing an inaudible word. He too could barely move, let alone speak. She squinted to read his lips. *Fire*.

Of course!

'Fire!' choked Sam with immense difficulty, as a serpentail wrapped around her neck.

Grandad looked at her with confusion.

'Fire!' she gasped, her voice strangled.

The penny dropped.

'Of course!' he yelled.

Grandad shoved the fire poker into a flaming sod

of turf. He bunged it into the flammable jam and that really got the flame going. He swung the flaming turf at the serpentails.

Mercifully, the deadly creatures loosened their grip on the children. They hissed in annoyance as Grandad charred and scarred the horrible bloodsuckers, but they did not yet retreat into the shadows. The old man continued until Sam was completely released and he made to free Sam's friends.

'Sam,' yelled Grandad, above the hissing. 'Why are serpentails hard to trick?'

For a moment, she was confused. She rubbed her neck to ease the throbbing pain. Then she understood.

A joke.

'I don't know. Why are serpentails hard to trick?'

'They have no legs to pull!' replied Grandad.

Sam laughed nervously.

Her (moderately) high-pitched laugh rang up through the room. All of a sudden, the serpentails stopped in their grasp, the sound of a child's laughter grating their ears (*extremely* difficult to find on their snake-like bodies).

Grandad had now freed Fisher and was working on Ivy and Wesley.

'What do serpentails say to loud children at the library?' shouted Sam. 'Sssssssss!'

Now Fisher laughed, louder than Sam had before. The serpentails began to cringe, as if in pain, as though the children's merriment had sapped their energy.

'A serpentail walks into a shop,' yelled Fisher. 'The shopkeeper says, "How did you do that?"'

Ivy and Wesley laughed loudly.

The serpentails were nearly limp, like rope.

'A sheep, two drums and a serpentail all fell over,' shouted Shepard. 'Baaa Dum Dum Tssss!'

Everyone laughed, including Shepard's sheep, 'Mmmmmmbaaahahahahahahaha!'

Like fingernails to a blackboard, the serpentails could not take the sound any longer. They disappeared under the furniture, into the shadows, completely out of sight.

'What do you call a serpentail that works for the government?' yelled Grandad, waving his flaming poker in the air. 'A civil serpentail!'

And Baker let out the wildest, most yodelling laugh above them all.

'HAAAHAHAHAHAHAHAHAHA HAHAHAHAA!'

Yes, Reader, in spite of their terrible jokes, their laughter worked a treat.

CHAPTER
14

That night was a lesson for Sam and all her classmates. Even Grandad.

Never let your guard down.

However, although it had been quite a traumatic event, the children were now even more determined to fight back. In fact, some of them even enjoyed the experience, most particularly Weaver who had to admit that it was the best (and only) sleepover he had ever been to.

Curiously, the more determined the children's resolve, the more and more frequently these monsters came. It was as though they had sensed their fight and looked to put a stop to it.

Still, the months passed and, despite all the unpleasantness, life was not all unpleasant. Sam had friends, a new pair of shoes which she protected vigilantly from the splochers (and Myrtle's opportunistic stomach), and all her teeth remained untouched by Major Chase's eager pliers.

The hunt for the monsters under the bed had become a major part of life for the children. Although they were now more vigilant than ever, this did not change their strategy. They had to sleep, but they were careful to arm themselves with the ultimate jam, and jokes, and nicknames, oh and of course candles next to their beds (though – ANOTHER DISCLAIMER – this is quite a dangerous tactic and not one that I recommend).

For now, injuries were minimal, although Shepard nearly had the wool pulled over her eyes by an unusually gassy and athletic splocher.

Grandad, too, seemed happy. Maybe it was Sam's company, or maybe he just felt extra refreshed by the water in his hip flask, but Sam liked to think it was their successful bludgeoning of the monsters which gave him a new lease of life.

THE END

Only kidding, Reader.

If it was that simple then we could all go and watch television, but I prefer reading. It's like star jumps for the mind.

Now, where was I? Ah yes, you could almost say, in a hushed and mumbled tone, that Sam was happy. Or at least, happi*er*. And of course, such being the case, it was only fitting that things should take a nasty turn.

Autumn had turned to winter and, with that, brought a thick blanket of snow to Draymur Isle. The island looked even more beautiful as blizzard after blizzard continued to sweep over the paths and fields and thatched rooftops. The children embraced the snow by having snowball fights and building snowmen (or splochermen, more accurately). Grandad put away his light summer cardigan in favour of his incredibly thick winter one. Soon it was the week leading up to Christmas and the scene looked appropriately festive.

Such were Grandad's spirits that he even decided to cut them a Christmas tree.

'You know, my dear,' he said as they set the tree a safe distance from the roaring fire (the first tree was too big), 'people used not to put Christmas trees inside.'

'Really?' asked Sam, brushing off the remaining snow from the branches. 'Then why do we do it?'

'The same reason we keep goats inside – it feels right to do so.'

The winter light was fading, and Grandad stared out the window as the heavy snow fell silently.

'Where are the Christmas lights, Grandad?' asked Sam.

'Hmm? Oh, they should be in those boxes.'

He walked across the room, limping every third step, and rummaged through the boxes that had in fact belonged to Sam's mother when she was a little girl.

But nothing.

'Where could they be? There was a big box full of Christmas lights right here.'

They both turned and looked at Myrtle, just in time to see the last of the electric wires vanish inside the greedy goat's mouth as if she was finishing off a delicious bowl of noodles.

Myrtle belched loudly, which was unbecoming of a dairy goat.

The goat licked her lips and stared back at them blankly.

Grandad rummaged through the boxes again.

'But this can't be,' he exclaimed in frustration. 'You just ate about ten thousand Christmas lights, you infuriating goat!'

Grandad gave chase, but there was no point. The Christmas lights were gone.

Sam laughed, while Myrtle sniffed curiously at a mouth-watering yard brush.

Soon, all of the decorations hung on the tree. There were very few so each made a difference.

'I think that's everything,' said Grandad.

'Nearly everything,' said Sam, who produced her mother's snow globe from her backpack. She shook it and placed it on the old mantelpiece above the fire.

A look of surprise flickered across Grandad's face.

'What is it, Grandad?'

'That belonged to your mother,' acknowledged Grandad with a sigh.

Sam nodded sadly.

'Did you know I made that for her when she was about your age?' he said. 'She loved it.'

The tiny lighthouse's light shone brightly while the snowflakes darted in every direction.

Chapter 14

'It must be nearly thirty years old,' said Grandad with a soft smile. 'It's hard to believe it still works properly after so many years.'

Sam did not blink; the sight was always spellbinding.

'I miss her so much, Grandad,' said Sam without thinking. 'I miss them both so much.'

Grandad put his arm around her and pulled her close. 'So do I, my dear,' he said.

There were few other words of comfort Grandad could offer. But he was there and that was enough.

'Now, tomorrow we shall try to get some more Christmas lights,' announced Grandad suddenly, clearing his throat. 'That is, of course,' he added, turning for Myrtle to hear, 'if there is any Christmas tree left to decorate!'

* * *

'Quick! Major Chase is coming!' Weaver shout-whispered across the classroom.

There was the usual urgent flurry of activity as Major Chase's footsteps could be heard coming down the corridor. Bits were shelved. Bobs were pocketed. And anything else was stored hastily inside their school desks.

Horace abruptly put a lid on a jar of their ultimate sticky jam, which he had taken to smearing on regularly like sun cream. Sam would have to wait until after class for her share of the protective jam.

She slammed shut a large notebook in which she'd been keeping a record of the children's nightly hunts. Not that they were in competition to see who could kill the most monsters. Actually, that's exactly what they were doing, Reader. A little competition is a healthy thing.

Major Chase appeared at the doorway and an abrupt stillness hit the room. A beam of winter's morning light shone in through the window, blinding most of the class.

The impeccably-groomed teacher stepped into the room in his three-piece suit and cape. His shoes shone black. His tie was tied to perfection. His pliers glistened eagerly.

'Good morning, class,' he said.

'Good morning, Major Chase,' replied the class, standing to attention, eyes forward, saluting as required.

Major Chase made his inspection slowly, his pristine shoes crossing the wooden floorboards. With a subtle wave, he gestured for the class to sit. He clasped his pliers with his right hand, inspecting for dust or deception with his left.

He reached the back of the room and circled behind Sam, peering down at the notebook on her desk.

'And what do we have here, Shipwright?' he demanded, needlessly loud, staring at the notebook which stood out from the normal copybooks in front of the other pupils.

'Nothing, sir,' said Sam, eyes forward.

Major Chase picked up the notebook and started reading.

'*Sam: 44 splochers, 17 serpentails. Horace: 36 splochers, 22 serpentails. Weaver: 14 ½ splochers, 19 serpentails, one very large, aggressive rat* . . . What is this meaning of all this, Shipwright?'

Sam hesitated a moment. 'It's a list, sir.'

'Well I can see it's a list, Shipwright,' he said, enraged. 'But a list of *what* precisely?'

She gulped before glancing up at him. 'A list of the monsters under the bed, sir.'

Major Chase frowned. 'A list of *what*?'

'It's a list of monsters that hunt children on the island, sir. We've been hunting *them* and . . . '

Sam read the room and shut her trap.

Major Chase turned pink and his eyes began to bulge. Sweat began to trickle from his perfectly-groomed moustache and a vein began to pulsate on his forehead as he continued to glow redder with rage.

His screams were heard three fields over, where crows took off in fright from the snow-covered branches.

'SHIPWRIIIGHT!' he roared. 'THAT. IS. IT!'

He dragged Sam from her seat to the top of the class (because teachers could do that back then). He took off his cape and his suit jacket and rolled up his sleeves. His perfect haircut flopped slightly with the sudden fury.

'You will learn . . . monsters under the bed . . . ' he muttered in blind rage before stepping forward, his pliers only a few inches from her face.

'What makes you think you can spread lies around here like that doddering grandfather of yours, hmm? Monsters under the bed do *not* exist. Monsters under the bed are made *up*. Monsters under the bed are *lies*.'

'She's telling the truth,' blurted Horace.

'They're real,' yelled Ivy.

'They want to eat children,' cried Wesley.

Major Chase's eyes looked as though they were about to jump from their sockets, he was so angry.

'Silence, all of you!' he snapped, raising his stunningly-polished pliers. 'Shipwright! Mouth *open*.'

Sam resisted, clamping her lips together tightly.

'Show me your teeth, Shipwright!' he roared.

'Major Chase?' came the shocked voice of the headmaster. Once again, Sam's choppers had been spared.

Major Chase stood up straight abruptly.

'Yes, headmaster, *sir*!' he said, eyes forward, forehead sweating.

Unbeknownst to Major Chase, the headmaster had seen everything from the doorway. He walked across the room and took the pliers from Major Chase who resisted for only a few short seconds.

'What is the meaning of this behaviour?' questioned the headmaster. 'Have I not told you before? No dental work during class time.'

'Yes, headmaster, *sir*!' replied Major Chase, arms by his side, standing to attention.

'Then what is this I see before me?'

'Shipwright, sir,' he replied, eyes straight ahead. 'She was speaking of monsters under the bed, sir. Spreading lies and fear.'

'Monsters under the bed?' asked the confused headmaster.

'Yes, sir! She was writing about them in her notebook, sir!'

The headmaster looked at the notebook in bewilderment. 'Oh, Major Chase,' tutted the headmaster, shaking his head. Then he turned to the class. 'Class, why don't you all go out into the playground?'

The children needed no further prompting and darted happily from their desks out into the snowy yard.

'Sam,' said the headmaster kindly. She looked up at him and saw her own reflection in his orange-tinted spectacles. 'My office, please.'

Horace hung back, giving her a look of sympathy, but there was nothing he could do for his friend.

The headmaster walked slowly from the classroom to his office, followed by Sam. They arrived at a polished wooden door at the other end of the corridor. On it sat a golden plaque which read, HEADMASTER'S OFFICE.

The headmaster opened the office door and gestured for Sam to enter first.

Chapter 14

'After you,' he said, smiling warmly at Sam.

She stepped into his office. It smelled of pipe smoke and reminded her of Grandad. It was a spacious square-shaped room. On one side sat a desk with a large antique globe next to it, with a tall bookshelf behind. A roaring fire waited at the other side of the room with a kettle for boiling water and two leather armchairs. Sam was instantly drawn towards the red-hot coals.

'Would you like a cup of tea, Sam?' asked the headmaster.

'Yes, please, headmaster,' she answered, inspecting an old chess set on a small table near the fire.

The pieces were made from a pale wood and the carving was simply beautiful. The detail looked impossible and, the closer Sam looked, the clearer it became. The pieces were moving. In particular, the queen's crown began to unravel before her very eyes. It almost resembled a serpentail . . .

Something felt wrong. Very wrong.

It happened quite suddenly. There was no warning.

From nowhere, Sam felt the unmistakable clench of a serpentail around her neck and she struggled to breathe.

The room went black.

CHAPTER
15

I *must be dead*, thought Sam.

    But if I can think, then I can't be dead, can I?

She was right.

Sam was not dead.

As her senses came back, she could feel a stiff coolness. There was no breeze at all, but there was a still and calm crispness.

Sam felt groggy and it took some time to regain full consciousness. She could hear the gentle lapping of tiny waves over pebbles only a few feet away. This stirred her further and she moved her head slightly.

She felt a bristliness against one side of her face, the side she had been lying on. She touched her hand to her cheek and breathed a split second sigh of relief – it was just grains of sand and tiny bits of shale.

Then she began to panic. *Where am I?*

She slowly lifted her head to find her bearings. She appeared to be on a beach, but it was dark. In fact, it was nearly pitch black.

How long have I been here?

As her eyes adapted, she realized where she was. Inside a cave.

The water in front of her was quite still and was in contrast to the choppy seas that she could see through the cavern's opening. It was clearly night-time.

There was a faint bluish glow all around. The cave had a jaggedness, like teeth, as some long rocks hung from the ceiling while others stood like spikes from the ground. The stench of seaweed and stale water was rancid.

Then, as she regained her vision fully, she saw them. And they saw her. And she had to rub her eyes once, twice and thrice because this could not be real.

Sam was gripped by terror, her worst nightmare coming true.

Splochers.

There were hundreds of them, all glaring at her.

Growling and foaming at the mouth like hungry wolves. They were slumped on the rocks like walrus (because, of course, they had no arms or legs), and were spread strategically all around the cave so that the only escape was through the still waters that led out into the stormy seas.

She sat up, which proved to be a mistake as the splochers began to growl and chant gruffly in unison, their sound echoing around the cave.

'*Crimmpler, crimmpler, crimmpler . . .*'

There was a thudding like a drum as the splochers reared and dropped rhythmically on the cave's floor. Their horribly aggressive growling seemed to match the beat.

Intense red eyes with a deathly stare.

Pale, green wrinkled skin that shone like slime.

Their teeth . . .

Their teeth stood out the most and filled Sam with a dread that she did not know could exist.

Armless, legless, slumped, they readied themselves for a gassy attack.

The sound of their gurgling, burbling, rippling,

bubbling bellies added to the unrest; they would blast, and pounce, and bite, and snipe at any second.

The growling continued, louder and louder and louder. Their mouths foamed sickeningly while their drool hung in long glutinous strands.

Yet not one splocher moved an inch. Sam could sense their impatience and she wondered why they held back.

'*Crimmpler, crimmpler, crimmpler . . .*'

'SILENCE!' came a wisping, high-pitched voice from behind Sam.

All of a sudden, a deathly stillness cut through the air.

The splochers no longer stared at Sam, but right past her. Suddenly, they were no longer interested in her. Instead their attention – or, more accurately, their complete and utter devotion – was for the source of the voice deep inside the cave.

Sam got to her feet but dared not move any further. She stared into the darkness from where the voice had come.

At first, she could see no one, then for one horrifying

moment, she thought she saw shadows whoosh by in the seemingly endless cavern, but these appeared to evaporate into nothingness. She peered further and was sure she could make out the vaguest of outlines lurking in the deepest darkness.

A voice came that swished and hissed like the wind. It rasped, and it grated, and it made the hairs on the back of Sam's neck stand on end.

'Saaaam. Shipwriiiiight,' came the unnerving voice again, and Sam's stomach lurched. Although quite softly spoken, it was high pitched, and jarring, and deeply unpleasant.

I've got to get out of here, Sam thought, but the only way out was through the water. She looked around frantically.

'It. Will. Not. End. Well. If. You. Run,' came the voice from the darkness and Sam tensed up.

Sam wracked her brains, struggling to think of what to say or what to do.

'I. Know. All,' it continued in a shriller tone, slightly louder, equally terrifying.

'The. Old. Man. Is. Not. Coming. For. You . . . He. Will. Never. Come. For. You . . . Like. The. Last. Child.'

'Like the last?' asked Sam, her mind racing.

'You. Belong. To. Mortempra. Sam. Shipwright.'

She knew that name. That name filled her with fear and made her sweat run cold.

'I need to go now,' said Sam, tears rising from her stomach to her throat and finally trickling from her eyes down her cheeks.

'You. Belong. To. Mortempra,' rasped the voice again.

Sam began to back away, but she had nowhere to go but the water behind her, and even then, the hundreds – if not thousands – of ravenous child-hungry splochers would make light work of her.

The wind in the cave suddenly picked up, seemingly from nowhere, swirling in amongst the hanging, spiking teeth.

Sam knew in her gut what this was before her, talking to her, almost taunting her. And as Grandad had taught her, always trust your gut.

It was a silentrap.

She was in grave danger and looked to stall what seemed like an inevitable attack.

'Why are you hiding away in there?' she shouted, her bravery shocking even herself.

Chapter 15

She listened . . . but nothing.

'I said, why are you hiding–?' she began, then paused. She could hear the sound of footsteps echo.

They were steady and grew louder as they got closer. *Tap . . . Tap . . . Tap . . .*

It seemed like a lifetime before Sam could make out the figure emerging from the darkness. But finally she saw it.

A baggy tweed suit and a black cape; fluffy white hair and rosy-red cheeks; faint-orange spectacles, even though there was no sunlight in here at all. 'Headmaster!' exclaimed Sam and for the briefest second, she let out a sigh of relief.

But the elderly man did not look himself. There was something missing. An emptiness. A deadness in his eyes.

'I. Hide. From. *Nothing,*' rasped the high-pitched voice now coming from the headmaster's mouth.

'What do you want?' asked Sam, her voice cracking.

'From. The. Shadows. I. See. Aaall,' rasped the voice. 'I. See. Your. Fiiiight . . . Your. Fight. Is. Futiiile.'

Sam's mind was racing.

Why would a silentrap possess an old man? she thought.

Splochers, serpentails and silentraps . . . they all hate adults. Unless . . .

A cold sweat hit Sam. *Unless the silentrap had taken the headmaster when he was a boy . . .*

Like a tonne of bricks, the realization hit her and the dots connected.

Grandad's brother had changed so suddenly in this cave all those years ago . . . Grandad had said he had not seen his Edgar since that day. But what if Edgar had never left the island? What if he had been taken by a silentrap?

'Edgar?' she asked fearfully.

The headmaster's eyes connected with Sam's for the first time since he had emerged from the back of the cave. The silentrap smiled knowingly through the headmaster. Through Edgar's body.

'Edgar. Is. Gone,' the voice continued. 'His. Body. Is. Old . . . I. Need. A. Neeeew.'

Sam's heart was pounding uncontrollably. She needed more time.

'I know what you are!' she blurted. 'You're a silentrap!'

The headmaster's body paused in its stride.

'I know what you do!' continued Sam. 'You possess children, but you don't scare me!'

The silentrap smiled slowly at first, then beamed broadly.

'I. Do. Not. Possess. Just. *Any*. Children . . . You. Are. The. *Special*. Child. You. Are. *Foooor*. Mortempraaaaa.'

The headmaster started to pace slowly towards her again.

'What is Mortempra though?' asked Sam, trying to stall for time.

'Mortempra. Is. Our. Queeeeen . . . I. Am. A. Part. Of. Mortempra's. Spirit . . . A Part. That. Roams. This. Island. For. Eternity . . . Mortempra. Must. Have. The. Special. Child. To. Break. The. Druid's. Curse.'

'Edgar!' shouted Sam, panicked. 'EDGAR! Remember Grandad, Edgar! Remember, Jacob, your brother!'

Before Sam could protest any further, the headmaster's cape began to move. For a moment, Sam thought that the headmaster was raising his arms to get his balance, and that maybe the silentrap was still not quite used to walking in his shoes, even after all these years.

But the headmaster's arms remained by its side.

Winding and slithering and sliding from the headmaster's cape, came one, then two, then three long and strong serpentails. Then four, then five, then six.

Sam froze. The serpentails wrapped around her ankles, and her feet seemed to sink into the sand below, as if she was being pulled beneath. The cave began to spin around her. It was as if she had been poisoned and her vision blurred in and out of focus.

Then a little voice called into her ear.

Snap out of it, Sam.

But the voice was not hers. Not man, nor silentrap, but boy.

Then it came again. Louder this time.

Sam, snap out of it!

Like a click of the fingers, Sam did as she was told. And as she came to, the room came back to her.

The headmaster's cold eyes still faced her, but she knew that voice; she knew who it was, willing her on. Willing her to escape. It was Edgar, encouraging her. From where, she did not know.

Remember what your Grandad taught you, Sam, the voice echoed kindly, but firmly. *Do what your Grandad told you. Trust your gut.* And as quickly as he had been there, he was gone.

The serpentails began to wrap more tightly around Sam's legs and the splochers' growling became even more heightened, their gassy rumblings growing even louder. Sam knew she had to respond, but she felt momentarily frozen.

Sam wondered if she had heard Edgar's voice at all as the snake-like vines made their way up her legs and torso towards her head, but she willed herself to resist. She had to concentrate.

Remember what Grandad said.

'There. Is. Noooo. Point. Fightiiiiing,' the silentrap mocked in its rasping voice.

Serpentails hate the sound of children's laughter.

While at that particular moment Sam did not feel like laughing one little bit, she had to try something, anything, as the serpentails were wrapping themselves tighter and tighter around her.

She thought of Myrtle eating the cheese sandwich on her arrival on the island.

The smallest glimmer of humour entered her belly.

'Hahahahahaha!' she cried unconvincingly. The serpentails' held their grip, although they did not tighten further.

Sam thought of Myrtle chasing Horace from the lighthouse for accidentally stepping on her hoof. She laughed loudly from her belly, this time the serpentails' grasp weakened slightly.

Sam thought of Grandad chasing Myrtle after the goat had polished off the Christmas lights like a delicious bowl of noodles. Her laughter echoed all around the cave and, finally, it seemed to work. The serpentails loosened their grip completely and the cruel vines retreated back towards the headmaster's, or more accurately, the silentrap's, cape.

Sam laughed triumphantly; she laughed like she meant it; she laughed for her life.

Then, she took a moment's breather.

This was a mistake.

The dead eyed headmaster looked directly into Sam's eyes and let out the most haunting call you could imagine. It was a call so loud and shrill and terrifying that Sam would never have believed it could have come from the old man's mouth.

'SEIZE HEEEEER!'

And the splochers held back no more.

CHAPTER
16

'Gets the crimmpler!' roared the largest of the splochers.

There was no doubt that this was the leader of the pack, as on its call, all the splochers advanced towards Sam.

Their bellies rumbled and thundered, and each began to release blasts of gas out their rear. Had they not looked so terrifying, Sam might have found their sounds quite amusing.

PFFFFFT!

BARP!

TOOT!

BbrrAAAAAAAP!

They were like a murderous army of farts, their war cry stinking up the cave.

Each advanced slowly as they had only one good gassy blast in them. After that, they had to build up enough steam to go again. But like many great packs in the wild, the splochers worked as a team. They were tactically placed around the cave so that Sam could not escape without entering the water. Worst still, Sam had not a teaspoon of jam on her.

After the shortest minute of Sam's life, one splocher was only a few feet away, then another needed just one good leap, and finally one splocher managed to blast right next to her feet, where it snapped at her foot. It clasped one of her shoes with its spiky jaw. It hurt tremendously. And once the splocher had Sam in its grip, it did not let go.

Sam screamed in pain.

As the other splochers exploded forward, Sam sensed that this was the end. However, the headmaster – Mortempra's silentrap – decided otherwise.

'Do. *Not*. Haaarm. Her . . . She. Hooolds. The. Druids'. Magic . . . Mortempra. Needs. Her. Whoooole!' hissed the headmaster.

For a moment, the splochers struggled to control themselves – they desperately wanted to feast on this

Chapter 16

juicy crimmpler. The growling continued louder and louder as each inched their way towards her. Some splochers even began to attack one another in agitation.

But the silentrap's voice was shrill above them all.

'DO. *NOT.* HARM. SAM. SHIPWRIGHT … THE. DRUID'S. MAGIC. IS. WITHIN … MORTEMPRA. NEEDS. HER. WHOOOOLE!'

Very, very, reluctantly, the splochers backed off, grumbling as they did. The headmaster appeared right next to Sam and, before she could react, a serpentail whipped from his cape, around her head to muffle her mouth and to avoid any more of her unbearable laughter. It was delicate as it wrangled her, though, seemingly saving her for something bigger.

The instruction was clear and even the splochers could understand. Sam was off limits. For now.

The headmaster walked from the sand into the water, the serpentails extending from his cape and wrapping Sam like a precious parcel. As the water reached knee height, he turned and faced her. Her heart beat faster and faster and the headmaster smiled a slow and satisfied smile.

'HOME!' hissed the silentrap suddenly, coldly.

Suddenly, all the splochers made for the water. They reminded Sam of gassy seals as they wriggled and exploded forward.

Upon entering the water, however, their movement changed altogether. Suddenly the splochers glided like sharks, each darting from the cave with purpose. And without any further delay, the headmaster was pulled into the water by the serpentails, as though *they* were in control and he was simply a piece of luggage. An empty vessel.

The serpentails dragged Sam and the headmaster through the water at a terrific pace. All around her swam splochers. Above. Below. Left. Right. Over. Under. Every which way a splocher soared in the whirling, twirling waters, the odd one darting in for a cheeky nip at her shoes or her jeans or her hoodie.

Almost as quickly as she had been pulled in, the serpentails catapulted her from the water and Sam shot out of the sea like a cannonball, high into the air. She was going at a staggering speed and was completely and utterly out of control.

As she reached the highest point of her catapult, her body slowed and she looked down. The vast white waves crashed mercilessly below and Sam inhaled a huge deep breath in anticipation of going under once again. But a serpentail plucked her from the air, placing her carefully on top of the rock that stood upright opposite the cave. She had circled this vast rock with Grandad and Myrtle on the boat when he had brought her to the cave before.

Opposite the rock, high above, stood the lighthouse on the cliff. She was agonisingly close to home.

The headmaster too had been set down at the very top of the grand sea stack, right opposite Sam. He immediately clenched her by the scruff of the collar with both hands so that Sam was forced to looked at the possessed headmaster and the silentrap staring back at her.

Sam could see the serpentails out of the corner of her eyes, slithering and weaving themselves from out of the sea. Very quickly, the rock was completely covered in the hissing, winding, snaky creatures. She felt a drag deep inside that glued her to the spot. She felt temporarily frozen, unable to move.

'Sam!' came a faint voice above all the racket.

It was a voice she recognized immediately.

A voice she would recognize anywhere.

Grandad.

Sam managed to look up at the lighthouse on the clifftop high above. There Grandad stood with all Sam's classmates: Horace, Ivy, Wesley, Baker, Cheeseman, Fisher, Slater, Shepard, Weaver, Major Chase. Wait, Major Chase? Even from down here in the dark she could see him ordering them all around like a real major, keen to ensure his platoon was all accounted for.

The headmaster now held Sam firmly by the throat, so firmly in fact that she found it difficult to breathe. He began to blow into Sam's face and, with that, the serpentail finally unravelled itself from around Sam's mouth.

The headmaster's breath began to glow a bluish silky colour.

Sam knew without being told that the silentrap was leaving Edgar's body in order to transfer itself into her. A small piece of Mortempra's spirit would enter her, *possess* her, just like it had possessed Edgar all those years ago. The bluish glow began to glide from the headmaster's mouth in through Sam's nose and mouth, entering Sam like it had with Edgar all those years before.

She began to feel dizzy.

And dizzier.

And dizzier and dizzier. So much so that she felt she would pass out at any moment.

This is it, she thought.

She was close to unconsciousness.

Then there was stillness.

Emptiness.

Complete blackness.

There was nothing there. No life. No hope.

The darkness was all-consuming.

But then from the dark there came the tiniest glimmer of light. A tiny speck. It was nearly nothing, but it was there and kept Sam aware.

Then came Edgar's voice once more.

Fight.

It came again. Louder this time.

Sam! FIGHT.

Sam opened her eyes and there he stood before her. Edgar. While his body was old, his eyes appeared youthful. The headmaster's hands still clasped her throat. The serpentails still covered the rock beneath their feet. The splochers still circled below and the stormy seas continued to swish and swirl violently. The silentrap continued to flow a blue, silky stream from Edgar's aged body in through Sam's mouth and nostrils.

But Sam and Edgar had a sudden connection above it all. All the other noise dulled and fell into the background. Above the sea, and the wind, and the splochers, and the serpentails, and the silentrap, it was just Sam and Edgar.

Don't let it take you like it took me, Sam, his voice echoed in her head. *Be brave.*

I'm so scared, Edgar.

There's no time for that, he said firmly. *Don't make the same mistake I made.*

But I don't know what to do!

Trust your gut. Let love's light be your guide.

What does that even mean? sobbed Sam.

They shared one last brief moment as Edgar's eyes twinkled knowingly, and then abruptly, sharply, fiercely, he seemed to roar,

FIIIIIGHT!

Like she had been hit by a jolt of electricity, Sam snapped back to life and all the noise came rushing back. The wind swirling. The splochers chopping. The serpentails hissing. The silentrap continuing to transfer itself into Sam. The bluish stream was constant in colour and grew stronger with each passing second. It was winning.

But Sam resisted.

If only she had something to fight with – what she wouldn't give for Horace's hatchet right now! Even a rock would do, but the ground was covered in serpentails and the headmaster's grip was too tight for her to move.

Frantically, she rummaged through her pockets.

Give me something. Anything.

Then she felt it.

Her mother's snow globe. It was a mystery how it got there. But she had no time to wonder. She considered Edgar's words.

Trust your gut. Let love's light be your guide.

With that, Sam stretched out her left hand and snatched off the headmaster's glasses. With her right hand, and with her last ounce of strength, she rapidly shook the snow globe and thrust it into the headmaster's eyes.

Like a blinding star, the globe shone brightly. So brightly that Sam could not look directly at it.

Brighter and brighter it shone.

Brighter. And brighter. And *brighter*.

The silentrap let out a long and harrowing wail before bursting from both Sam and Edgar, exploding into a magnificent *FLASH!*

The power inside the snow globe was nearly too great to contain. Sam's hands shook with the effort to hold it steady. It vibrated faster and for a moment she thought it too would explode. But the tighter she held it, the calmer the snow globe became, until finally the light faded and they were all cast back into darkness. Sam and the headmaster stood next to one another, just as they had a moment before.

Except now there was silence and, as Sam looked into the headmaster's eyes, she saw no silentrap, no man, but a child-like stare. Edgar's body was frail, but his eyes were young, scared, lost, and confused. Bewildered, disorientated, panicked, the old man searched around.

Then he saw what he was looking for, up high on the clifftop next to the lighthouse where stood Grandad.

The headmaster let out a cry so loud and clear that Sam thought it could be heard in space. And it was not a man's but a child's voice that rung through the air that night:

'JACOB!'

Sam looked up at the clifftop to see Grandad, and even from that far away she could see the utter shock on her grandfather's face.

Without further hesitation, the great man dived off the vast cliff into the treacherous seas far, far below. He would not let his little brother go again.

Grandad was coming for his Edgar.

CHAPTER
17

G randad plunged into the water with the grace of a retired Olympic swimmer. The old dog had learnt his tricks many years before.

But while Grandad may have had a frame like a door, he looked tiny in the vast waves that swayed back and forth between the upright rock and the base of the cliff.

Back and forth, back and forth, the white water chopped and fizzed, and Sam watched on fearfully as Grandad's head bobbed like an apple.

'Where's he gone?' shouted the headmaster, frightened, teary-eyed. 'Jacob! JACOB!'

The headmaster's voice had returned to normal. But he was not at all as he had been. The silentrap was gone, but the headmaster was not himself. At least, not as Sam knew him.

Then it hit her. This was *not* the headmaster as she knew him, but Edgar. And Edgar was old in body only. The silentrap had hit pause on his life like a cruel DJ. Sam saw before her not the elderly headmaster, nor a silentrap, but the oldest looking boy she had ever seen (including her second cousin, Joe, who started shaving when he was eight).

Yes, it was insanity, but Sam knew it to be true. Here stood Edgar the boy. And he was scared.

'I can't see him!' shouted Edgar, searching frantically. 'Where's he gone?'

Sam and Edgar desperately surveyed the water. Aside from the white waves, it was almost pitch black, which made it incredibly hard to see.

'There he is!' yelled Sam suddenly, and true enough, Grandad was steadily making his way towards them, his gasping head would emerge from one particularly powerful wave before dipping immediately back under another.

Arm after arm, Grandad struggled against the current. He moved painfully slowly, at times struggling to make any forward progress at all. But he kept at it. He couldn't give up.

Edgar began to climb hurriedly down the huge rock to meet him, clambering over the serpentails that seemed strangely limp and lifeless. It was as if they had been stunned and subdued by the snow globe's powerful light.

'Edgar, be careful!' called Sam, clambering after him. She was worried that the baggy tweed pants and long black cloak would cause the OAP (Odd Aged Pensioner) to trip. As Edgar reached the rock's bottom, the waves crashed heavily, soaking him to the skin. But he clearly could not have cared less. Grandad got closer and Edgar outstretched his arm. The waves threatened to sweep Grandad away at any second.

'Grab hold, Jacob!' cried Edgar. 'Quick!'

The splochers in the water were also subdued, but then again Grandad was not a child and would probably have tasted like vomit to them.

Finally, Grandad grabbed his brother's hand with his left hand and dragged himself up onto the base of the great rock with his right, the waves lapping heavily and relentlessly in behind him. It took him a moment on all fours to catch his breath before he looked up.

Now that Edgar was free of the silentrap, which had possessed him beyond the point of recognition to his loved ones, Grandad finally saw his Edgar before him. A spell had been lifted. A curse had been broken.

'All these years,' said Grandad, standing as the waves crashed loudly around them, 'they all said I was crazy . . . I thought I'd lost you forever.'

'I'm sorry, Jacob,' wept Edgar. 'I tried to escape, I tried so hard, but it wouldn't let me go.'

The two drenched pensioners embraced tightly, water streaming down their weary-lined faces. Sam was unsure

if it was tears or salt water, but it didn't really make a difference, after all, both taste the same.

Edgar looked at his frail hands, the reality of a lost life hitting home. Grandad placed his arms warmly around his shoulders and kissed his little brother's head.

Another moment passed and the waves and the wind were worsening.

'Home,' Grandad declared. He nodded resolutely at them both. 'Edgar, Sam, let's go.'

Sam carefully put the snow globe back into her pocket.

'What's that on you?' asked Edgar, inspecting Grandad's cardigan.

'*Myrtle's Ultimate Sticky Jam for Keeping Monsters Away*. It's very hard to wash off!' confirmed Grandad. Because, even though he did not strictly speaking need the ultimate protective jam, he liked to be involved. 'That reminds me. Sam, put some more of this on, quickly.'

Sam dumped a jar of the ultimate jam all over her head and eagerly began to scrub it into her hair and onto her hoodie and jeans and shoes.

Grandad was first to dive back into the rough water,

then Sam. But Edgar hesitated at the sight of the splochers, even though they too, like the serpentails, appeared rather subdued.

'It's okay, I've got you,' reassured Grandad. 'Just hold on to me and you'll be fine.'

The three held on tightly to one another.

'Keep kicking your legs!' shouted Grandad as the waves pressed them back against the rock at first. 'Don't stop!'

The small human triangle swung and topped and turned on the tall waves. It was a great struggle, but they kept going. Thankfully, the splochers had no interest in them as Grandad and Edgar's bodies were tainted by age, while Sam was covered in jam that would have tasted like incredibly sticky ear wax to them.

'Keep going!' yelled Grandad. 'Not far to go! We'll have some celebration tonight!'

They were getting closer to the cliff face now, when suddenly,

FWEEEEEET!

What was that sound? Then it came again, louder.

FWEEEEEET!

Then Sam recognized it. The loudest and most piercing whistle this side of the moon. Shepard's whistle.

FWEEEEEEEEET!

Horace, Ivy, Wesley, Slater, Cheeseman, Fisher, Baker, Weaver, Shepard (with about a half a dozen sheep) and Major Chase all stood atop the cliff.

'Incoming!' yelled Major Chase in his outdoor voice (which was very loud indeed, Reader).

With that, Fisher produced a huge fishing rod which could have been used to fish for sharks in the deep seas.

Or sunken ships in the deeper seas.

Or aliens in outer, outer, outer space.

Fisher stepped forward with Major Chase and the rest of Sam's classmates either side, helping him cast a gigantic fishing line back and forward.

'That's it,' instructed Major Chase. 'Quickly, now!'

With that, the line was cast the entire way down the cliff face (which was about the height of a very modest skyscraper).

Sam did not know where they could have possibly found a line long and strong enough to extend the whole way down. But as it slapped hard into the water, she realized what it was.

SLAP!

A serpentail.

A very, very long one. A very, very dead one.

Grandad grabbed hold of the line and wrapped it around his arm, the suckers clasping naturally onto him, working perfectly to lock him in.

'Quickly!' yelled Grandad. 'Grab on!'

Sam and Edgar did just that, and not a moment too soon.

'ONCE, TWICE, THRICE!' roared Major Chase (very, *very* loudly), and with that they *heaved* on the serpentail fishing rod.

The lifeless elastic serpentail abruptly reefed them from the water, and up towards the top of the cliff at an astonishing speed.

CHAPTER
18

Like a backwards bungee jump, Sam, Grandad, and Edgar flew up through the cold night air.

They were going so fast that Sam felt her face stretch backwards and her eyes bulge widely.

Before she knew it, they had torn right past the island's cliff edge altogether, high up into the air. As they landed back on the island, thankfully, a thick blanket of snow cushioned their fall.

OOF!

(Well, sort of.)

The three lay in a heap like three dishevelled rugs, but there was no time to lie about. They were soaked to the skin, and shivered tremendously, but they were in great spirits.

Major Chase and Sam's classmates quickly gathered around them.

'Headmaster!' called Major Chase, helping Edgar to his feet. 'Are you all right, sir? When Hatchet told me Shipwright was missing I . . .'

'Who are you calling *sir*?' asked a confused 10-year-old Edgar. 'Why are you speaking so loudly?'

For the first time in a long time, Major Chase was rather lost for words.

'What are you wearing, sir?' asked Sam, taking advantage of her teacher's rare silence.

Major Chase was dressed head to toe in his full dress army uniform, complete with white gloves, peaked cap and polished medals.

'I'm ready for battle, Shipwright!' he said proudly. 'They all laughed when Major Gregory Widdlethorn Chase turned up on the island with a car boot full of weaponry, but who's laughing now?'

The group stared at Major Chase with a look of confusion, as if trying to figure out a particularly tricky riddle.

Sam explained all that had happened in the cave.

'Hang on a second!' said Wesley, grinning widely. 'The headmaster is a ten-year-old boy? What's your favourite type of sweet then?'

'Oh, definitely a bag of bumbleswishers,' smiled Edgar. 'They fizz on your tongue before going all sweet and gloopy.'

'What's a bumbleswisher?' asked Ivy.

'What? They don't make bumbleswishers any more?' asked Edgar, quickly turning to face Grandad who shook his head sadly.

'Candykiddlers?' asked an alarmed Edgar.

Grandad avoided Edgar's gaze.

'Chocolate wazzlers?'

No reply.

'No, no, no!' exclaimed Edgar. 'You're telling me they don't make doddle-doodle beans any more? Or sludgy squitchybottoms? Or pundle raspers?'

Grandad's silence said it all.

'Awww, not pundle raspers too!' said Edgar, his face covered by both hands as if life was not worth living any more.

Before there was time to comfort him, there came a

noise so loud that at first Sam thought it must have been thunder–

BOOM!

–and she waited for a flash of lightning. But none came.

Then again the noise sounded, even louder this time.

BOOM!

Sam turned and stared back down at the sea stump on which they had stood minutes earlier. The huge, upright rock had split right in half, top to bottom, like a nut's shell.

What rose from the split rock was unlike anything Sam had ever seen before.

It was neither beast nor monster, but a black and ominous cloud that spilled from within the crack and began to rise up with purpose. It moved like a silk sheet, spreading wider and wider the higher it soared, soon blocking out the moon and the stars. While it took no real form, there was life to it. The wind suddenly picked up and howled all around them.

'What is that?' yelled Sam.

'It's Mortempra's spirit rising!' yelled Edgar, the voice of experience. 'All the evil that happens on this island; it all comes from Mortempra!'

'We're in danger!' shouted Grandad.

Suddenly Sam had a lightbulb moment . . . Literally.

'The lighthouse!' she yelled. 'It was the light that released Edgar! Maybe the light will defeat Mortempra!'

'It's worth a try!' shouted Edgar above the racket.

The group fought their way through the howling wind and deep snow.

Step by step, the lighthouse grew closer.

Fifty feet.

Forty feet.

The lighthouse was now just a stone's throw away.

By the skin of their toenails, the group bundled inside.

'Grandad, do we have any old bulbs for the beacon's light?'

'Under the hatch!' he shouted above the noise of the lighthouse, which rattled and creaked with the wind.

'Move!' cried Sam, storming between Major Chase and Wesley.

She heaved the kitchen table out of the way and pulled open the hatch door. Unsurprisingly, she had to pull out jar after jar of random jam to get through.

Diet jam, jam-free jam, no-added-sugar jam . . . what's that, Reader? Right, not the time . . .

Sam's classmates formed a human chain and quickly the hatch area below was cleared of jam.

Sam jumped down into the space below the trap door. The boxes were many and dusty, but she quickly found an *enormous* light bulb. It was awkward in both size and shape. It would take some patience to get it back through the little hatch door above, and they did not have the time for that.

Fortunately, Horace Hatchet was on hand to assist, hacking at the floorboards. Wesley too was there to support, by which I mean demolish much of the floor with a nearby axe. The wood-chopping frenzy continued for only a few moments as Sam's other classmates also helped the cause, using some good old-fashioned brute force. Grandad was probably the first person in history to be pleased about a gang of youths tearing up his home.

As the hatch extension neared completion, Sam covered her eyes to avoid stray splinters.

'Quick,' she yelled from below, 'we've got to get this plugged in upstairs!'

With some struggle, the classmates shifted the bulb carefully through the widened hatch and up the winding stairs to Sam's room at the very top of the lighthouse. Sam glanced out the window and could see the sky was still void of the moonlight and the stars.

While the bulb was heavy, it felt as though something else was weighing them down. Something deep inside them that they could not place.

But they kept going. They *had* to keep going.

The class placed the bulb down on Sam's bedroom floor and looked above her bed at the ceiling. The beacon's light socket was far too high for them to reach.

This was Slater's time to shine. 'We've got to build a human pyramid!'

Shepard rolled her eyes.

'All right, let's do it!' said Sam. 'But quickly!'

Slater hastily got to work. He ordered the largest of the group – Grandad, Edgar, and Major Chase – onto on all fours; they would be the base of the pyramid.

Then, in order of size, he added the next level, and the next. Weaver, the smallest of the group would be at the top, and he took great pleasure in stepping on Major Chase's hands and head as he climbed. He stood atop the pyramid and, panting with the effort, shimmied the lightbulb into the socket.

Nothing happened. They remained in darkness.

Mercifully, however, the bulb buzzed, then flickered as if waking up, and within seconds its light shone brightly across the bay. Sam breathed a moment's sigh of relief.

But as she stared up at the sky, she realized that the draping black mist above had become thicker. It now resembled black ink rather than a cloud. It spilled above like a blanket and the wider it spread, the greater its hold became on the island.

Suddenly a cold, callous breathing began to sound all around them.

It was wheezing.

But it was not the sound of weakness. It was the sound of amusement.

Laughter.

Horrible, wheezing, rasping laughter.

The laughter began to reverberate all about them, as if mocking their efforts. It echoed like a speaker in an old train station. Sam found it entrancing and could not tell how long it went on for, such was its allure.

HAHAHAHAHAHAHAHAHAHAHAHAHAHAHA HAHAHAHAHAHAHAHAHAHAHAHAHA HAHAHAHAHAHAHAHAHAHAHAHAHAHA . . .

Suddenly there came another noise from behind her.

A recognizable noise.

Engines.

Lots of engines.

She glanced out the window towards Draymur Isle's small village and saw lights: dozens of them approaching the lighthouse. And fast.

CHAPTER
19

'What is that?' exclaimed Fisher, squinting against the glaring lights.

Down through the steep field and heavy snow came a grand procession of tractors, cars, vans, and some bicycles too, their headlights piercing the darkness.

'It's our parents!' yelled Horace, spotting his father's butcher van. 'They must have seen the lighthouse's light shining and come to help.'

The tyres halted; the vehicle doors opened; the bottoms dismounted the bicycles.

The gang hurried down the stairs and out into the snow. Before they could fill their parents in, Horace's father started on one of his rants.

'Horace Henry Herman Tony Hatchet!' he roared.

Chapter 19

'What do you think you're doing here? I told you to steer clear of this madman!' he shouted, pointing at Grandad.

'But he's been telling the truth all this time, dad!' replied Horace. 'Monsters under the bed *are* real! They exist!'

'Absolute nonsense!' said Horace's dad, turning to the other parents who nodded approvingly. 'We've all heard the legend! We all know that monsters were banished from this island long ago and this lunatic is spreading lies.'

'He's not lying—' argued Horace.

'You've said quite enough,' interrupted his father. 'It's straight to *Butcher Billy's Butcher Academy for Butchering Children* with you! Headmaster, you of all people must understand. What have you to say?'

Edgar had been watching the back and forth like it was a particularly aggressive table tennis tournament. He stood open-mouthed, unsure of what to say.

'Monsters are real and they're led by an evil spirit called Mortempra,' shouted Sam, growing particularly impatient, 'and she's hunting children!'

'You've got to believe us,' cried Ivy.

'*I'll* be hunting children if you two don't get over here right now!' Ivy and Wesley's mother hissed at the twins.

'What do you think that is?' asked Sam. 'Where do you think the moon has disappeared to? Where are the stars? It's Mortempra. Didn't you hear her laugh as you drove here?'

'We're sick of this,' yelled Shepard's mother at Grandad. 'We're woken up in the middle of the night by that cracked lighthouse of yours, only to find our children are not in their beds! And why? Because they're running around with some doddery old fool!'

Grandad stood silently, knowing that any objection was pointless.

'It's no surprise,' Slater's father chimed in, shaking his head. 'He's always encouraging bad behaviour!'

'Always spreading rumours,' added Fisher's mother.

'Always weaving lies,' said Weaver's father.

Suddenly, the wind picked up and all present could hear that horrible raspy laughter ring up through the air once more. This time the adults gathered could no longer deny that they'd heard it.

HAHAHAHAHAHAHAHAHAHAHAHAHAHAHAHAHA HAHAHAHAHAHAHAHAHAHAHAHAHAHA HAHAHAHAHAHAHAHAHAHAHAHAHAHA ...

Suddenly, with a *CRACK!* the lighthouse light blew and went out.

'Just an old fuse, I'm sure,' said Horace's father, slightly nervously. 'Nothing to worry about.'

But then, one by one, all of the car headlights blew, and the crowd was thrown into a deep darkness.

As their eyes adapted, finally they stared up at the giant blanket of inky clouds and wispy shadows. It was so large that it seemed to cover the entire island and beyond. It felt alive, as if pressing down upon them, its threat imminent.

Or rather, Mortempra's threat was imminent.

Sam glanced back at the village nervously. Curiously, no windows were lit. There was no light whatsoever in fact. The darkness was total.

'What *is* that?' asked Baker's mother, suddenly startled.

Horace's father gaped, clearly trying to make sense of it. 'Well, clouds, I mean ... ' he began nervously. 'Clouds are always changing ... '

'Not the cloud,' said Baker's mother. 'I mean what is *that*?' She looked as though she had seen a ghost.

Sam looked in the same direction as her, back towards the cliff edge and gasped.

There stood a ginormous splocher.

A splocher about the size of Horace's father's butcher van.

A splocher illuminated by Mortempra's presence so that all present could now clearly see.

It was a symbol of power; a show of Mortempra's strength.

It growled aggressively, its mouth foaming, its snot-coloured skin glistening, its eyes glowing red.

And it was not alone.

Another splocher appeared over the cliff edge . . . and another, and another. More and more splochers appeared, yet how they could have climbed Sam did not know because they slumped forward clumsily with each movement.

Some were large, some were small. But they all had one thing in common.

They were hungry.

Very, very hungry.

The children's parents gasped in horror at the splochers coming up over the cliff. They froze in terror.

'Gets those **crimmplers!**' roared the mini-van-sized splocher.

Just as inside the cave, the splochers' bellies rumbled and thundered and each began to release blasts of gas out their rear.

They began to advance slowly, but with great ambition.

And they chanted as they advanced.

'*CRIMMPLER . . . CRIMMPLER . . .*'

The splochers were not alone either.

Sam could hear a nasty, deadly hissing that was all too familiar.

HISSSSSSSSSSSSSSSSSSSSSSSSSSSS SSSSSSSSSSSSS!

Over the cliff edge, from the direction of the split sea stack, the serpentails appeared in their droves. And like the splochers, they advanced with one thing on their mind. They were thirsty and needed urgent refreshment.

More and more serpentails raced past the splochers and straight for the children.

The adults shrieked wildly as the deadly vines slinked

towards the lighthouse. Horace's father looked as though he might pass out with fear.

'They're coming for *us*!' yelled Sam, facing her classmates. 'We've got to fight back!'

'There's too many,' cried Ivy.

'She's right, Sam!' shouted Horace. 'There's no way we can take on that lot ourselves, even with our tricks.'

Major Chase cleared his throat to get their attention.

'Shipwright, I'm ready for battle. And, as I was saying, they all laughed when Major Gregory Widdlethorn Chase turned up on this island with a car boot full of weaponry. But who's laughing—'

'Will you get to the point?' snapped Edgar.

'Yes, sir. Of course, *sir*!' said Major Chase, standing stiff to attention, saluting his superior. 'Quickly, to the boot of my car!'

The group scurried quickly to Major Chase's nearby car. He opened the boot and the class stood slack-jawed at the sight before them.

In Major Chase's boot was an enormous cannon (along with some highly questionable dentistry tools). He pressed a button tucked away nicely in the corner of the car. An electronic whirring noise sounded and the cannon began to rise on a platform. It came to a stop at about Sam's head height.

'Help me, now. Quickly!' instructed Major Chase, and the group helped swivel the cannon in the direction of the oncoming splocher and serpentail attack.

The decorated war teacher began to prepare the cannon. 'Now, normally I'd use gunpowder and a few cannonballs . . . and maybe some false teeth . . . but I'm not sure that will work with this lot.'

'Jam,' shouted Sam. 'We've tonnes of it in the lighthouse!'

'Brilliant, Sam,' yelled Grandad.

'Don't forget to use *Myrtle's Ultimate Sticky Jam for Keeping Monsters Away*!' shouted Horace.

'It's flammable too,' said Fisher with a grin. 'The serpentails won't like that!'

The group got right to it, forming another human chain, passing jar after jar of jam to Weaver who stood alongside Major Chase, acting as his assistant.

'That's it, Weaver, there's a good lad, let's try a jar of normal, apple pie jam to start!'

Weaver plonked a large pie-shaped jar of jam into the cannon and Major Chase lit the fuse. The jar of jam took flight, a bit like a grenade, smashing into the splochers, which shrieked wildly, the hot apple burning the tongue of the giant splocher, who howled like a little baby splocher.

'Hohooo, wonderful,' said Major Chase, clapping. 'Let's try something stronger!'

Into the cannon went some of *Myrtle's Ultimate Sticky Jam for Keeping Monsters Away.*

BOOM . . .

Fisher was not lying! It was the most flammable jam ever invented. All it needed was the tiniest spark and it burst into flames mid-air, splatting down onto the oncoming serpentails (who were also very flammable by the looks of it, Reader).

Very quickly the island was illuminated as fireball after fireball of jam flew across the night sky.

Major Chase's cannon was incredibly accurate.

However, Mortempra's monsters continued to swarm over the cliff edge in large numbers. There appeared to be no stopping them.

Splocher, after splocher, after splocher; serpentail, after serpentail, after serpentail.

But Sam and her classmates would not give up. They could not give up, and the cannon boomed again and again and again, as their parents looked on in horror.

And it was not just jam that was being fired at the enemy. Everyone desperately added whatever they could find to the pile of ammunition.

Grandad found some spare coal.

Edgar found some rocks.

Fisher found some fish guts.

BOOM . . . BOOM . . . BOOM . . .

Slater found some old slates.

Weaver threw in his rusted brace mask (much to Major Chase's dismay).

Baker found some fresh dough (which flattened a splocher into a sploch pot pie).

BOOM...BOOM...BOOM...

Horace threw in a spare hatchet.

Shepard threw in some spare wool.

Even Cheeseman, with some hesitancy, sacrificed some gooey Camembert.

BOOM...BOOM...BOOM...

The effort was outstanding, but still Mortempra's monsters did not let up. Like a broken tap, their stream was relentless.

Each time the courageous group pushed the monsters back, the splochers blasted forward and the serpentails slid closer. Even the children's forced laughter could not stall the serpentails whose hissing was far too loud, and drowned out the children's attempts.

Soon, the monsters had them surrounded. Sam and her classmates had nowhere to hide as they stood with their backs to the lighthouse.

And through it all that high-pitched laughter rang

through Sam's mind, and the closer the monsters came, the louder the laugh became, until it drowned out every other sound.

HAHAHAHAHAHAHAHAHAHAHAHAHAHAHAHA HAHAHAHAHAHAHAHAHAHAHAHAHA HAHAHAHAHAHAHAHAHAHAHAHAHAHA . . .

Sam began to feel dizzy.

She felt so dizzy that she began to sway, and her vision blurred in and out of focus.

The cold, callous breathing returned. Strangely, however, it now felt soothing to her. She felt as if she were about to fall into a deep sleep, and all the surrounding sounds were taken completely.

Mortempra's words flowed gently into Sam's ears.

The voice was neither cold nor raspy, but warm and kind . . . and very familiar.

It was a voice that Sam had not heard for a long time; a voice that Sam had longed to hear every day and every night; a voice that she missed desperately.

Her mother.

'Come to Mortempra, Sam.'

Sam looked up at the dark inky cloud that hung above.

It began to twist, and swish, and morph, and hiss. Suddenly it was not a blanket, but a veiled woman that swept and swirled in the blackness high above, and Sam felt drawn towards her.

And with each passing second, the inky cloud morphed more and more into focus, until Sam recognized clearly the sight above.

Sam's mother was exactly as she remembered her.

She spoke kindly, 'Give in to Mortempra and we shall be together. Give in to Mortempra and we shall never be apart again.'

Sam needed no further invite. She let go and allowed herself drift towards her mother's voice. Heck, she would have sprinted if she could. There was nowhere else she wanted to be but in her mother's arms. She did as she was told.

Her head began to spin; her mind swished and swirled, and the weight of her body became too much to bear.

She fell into a bitter darkness.

And she fell, and she fell, and she fell.

And she fell.

And she fell.

And she fell.

Chapter 19

I'd like to tell you that it was all okay, Reader. I'd like to tell you that the group miraculously escaped and that Mortempra and all her monsters were banished back to where they came. I'd like to tell you that Edgar got his childhood back.

More than anything, I'd like to tell you that this was all just a dream. That Sam awoke in her bed and this had all been a nightmare.

But this was worse than your very worst nightmare. It was a horrifying reality. And in reality, sometimes things do not always work out. Of all people, Sam knew this to be true.

She had no more fight left to give, no more fight *worth* giving.

She gave herself to Mortempra.

But.

But from the darkness, there shone the tiniest speck of light, so tiny that it barely existed. A fleck only; the faintest sparkle. But it was there . . . just.

Hope.

Hope.

It got bigger. And bigger still. AND BIGGER STILL.

And it was not just one light coming for her, but a series of multi-coloured lights.

Like Christmas decorations; like Christmas lights.

What appeared to be a multi-coloured shooting star came galloping towards her, growing ever faster and getting ever closer. And as it did, Sam felt the bite of the cool night air against her cheeks. And she was overcome with a stark relief because she knew that she could feel something again.

Then all her senses came back, one by one.

She could feel Grandad's hand in hers. She could smell the lighthouse's smouldering, smashed light. She could hear the faint shuffling, and shouting, and hissing, and growling of Mortempra's monsters. Finally, her vision came back to reveal the most oddly beautiful sight she had ever seen.

Like a guardian angel coming to vanquish Mortempra, a majestic creature came storming down the long hill sloping towards them.

Myrtle.

CHAPTER
20

The manic goat dashed downslope at a fantastic speed.

But she was not herself. Or at least, she was not as she had been.

She sparkled different colours: gold and green, and red and silver, and purple and pink.

And as she grew closer, she could be heard yelling.

'MMMBAAAAAAAAAAAAA!'

She was angry.

Very angry.

Very, very angry.

'MMMBAAAAAAAAA!'

And as Myrtle screamed, she began to emit a colourful beam of light.

The great goat's hooves could be heard galloping down the slope towards the lighthouse. They made a satisfying *TU-LOT! TU-LOT!* thudding sound atop the powdery snow.

'The Christmas lights!' cried Grandad. 'That infuriatingly glorious goat must have eaten about ten thousand Christmas lights!'

And as the hooves got louder, her yell got louder.

She looked profoundly fearsome, yet equally majestic. Almost saintly. Angelic. Perfect.

Myrtle's galloping almost slowed down, as if she were running in slow motion so that Sam could see every last detail. Her screaming breath beamed brighter and more colourful with each step so, like a great ray from a multi-coloured torch, it shone over all of the splochers and all of the serpentails who began to growl and hiss in rage. Even though their numbers far outweighed the lone goat, Myrtle's multi-coloured light was too powerful for them.

The magnificent goat continued her gallop. She was nearly at the bottom now, and she was absolutely livid.

She gave a yell that was so loud, and emitted a light so bright and colourful from her mouth, that all the splochers and the serpentails were flung back off the island and into the sea.

'MMMMMBAAA AAAAA!'

With Myrtle's last gasp, with her last ounce of strength, the screaming beam flashed white, forcing all the islanders to block their eyes with both hands. The ground tremored violently and, for a moment, Sam felt the island would open up and swallow them whole.

But what followed was a perfect stillness, calm and pure.

Sam could still hear Myrtle's cry ringing through her ears, but as the white light evaporated, the night turned to day and that's where it stayed. And the beautiful goat was gone.

But there was peace.

No splochers.

Chapter 20

No serpentails.

No silentraps.

No Mortempra.

Total tranquillity.

As the sun rose, Sam was certain she could hear Myrtle's yells echoing in the wind growing ever fainter, until there was no sound at all but for the surrounding sea that crashed and swirled against the rocks of their exposed island.

The sunrise shone gold and green, and red and silver, and purple and pink. For several moments, no one moved a muscle. The islanders stood captivated by the beauty of the sky, the likes of which none of them had ever seen before, and some were unlikely to ever see again.

Sam was first to break the silence. 'Where's Myrtle?!'

She sprinted towards the cliff edge (or as best she could in the thick snow which came up to her knees). Sam's classmates, Grandad, Edgar, and Major Chase followed.

The large sea stack which had been split in half now appeared unscathed.

The group stood speechless.

'But . . . where did they all go?' pressed Sam. 'The splochers and serpentails! Where did Mortempra go?'

She stared up at the morning sky. The black, inky cloud was nowhere to be seen.

She looked down at the white waves that crashed around the sea stack, her thoughts swishing in her mind.

'I don't understand,' said Sam. 'What happened?'

'Mortempra is a source of immense evil magic, Sam,' said Edgar. 'You showed a special power tonight.'

'What power?'

'As I've told you, my dear,' said Grandad, 'you are descended from druids. The most magical and powerful of all people. There is a magic in you somewhere, I have no doubt.'

Sam thought about this for a moment. 'Something weird happened on the sea stack with the snow globe,' she said slowly. 'Wait . . . how did the snow globe get into my pocket?'

Grandad and Edgar looked at one another and smiled, seemingly happy to leave the question unanswered.

'And how did you all know where I was after I was brought to the headmaster's office?' Sam continued.

'We waited in the yard for you and when you didn't

show, I told Major Chase,' Horace replied. 'When he saw you and the headmaster were both missing, he insisted that we go and see your Grandad. We searched everywhere for you. Then your Grandad remembered the cave. We were about to go down there when we saw you from the cliff, on top of the sea stack.'

'But why were we taken to the sea stack?' Sam asked. 'Why didn't the silentrap just try to possess me in the cave?'

'Because Mortempra cannot land on the island,' Edgar replied. 'That is a crucial part of the curse. It takes very powerful magic for a silentrap to move from one body to the next. Only Mortempra herself could make that happen – and she needed the *right* child. I believe that is why she possessed me for so long. And I believe that she was on the sea stack with us tonight in her truest possible form.'

Sam stared into Edgar eyes. She felt she knew him well even though they had only just met, as if they had a connection.

'And when we were communicating, on the sea stack . . . it was telepathic, wasn't it? We didn't need to speak aloud at all.'

Edgar nodded.

'I'm quite sure that is the druid blood we share. An ability stored deep within, perhaps only to be used when we truly need it.'

There were many more questions bouncing around Sam's mind, but Grandad wrapped an arm around her. 'Tell me what I want to hear, Sam.'

For a moment, she had no clue what he meant.

'Your nickname, Sam,' he reminded her.

Sam smiled. 'It's me, Cane. Myrtle's Beard.'

He nodded at her and stared out at sea. 'I shall miss Myrtle's beard. I shall miss her very much.'

The group looked out at sea for a long time that morning, hoping perhaps that Myrtle would reappear.

But she never did.

The short-tempered goat had sacrificed herself for something bigger. And Sam knew it.

They say that three is the magic number, Reader. Sam's close family had always been that way. First, with her mum and dad. Then, with Grandad and Myrtle. And now, with Grandad and Edgar.

I suppose you'd like to hear what happened next.

Well, for one, Grandad was owed a lot of apologies.

Chapter 20

The islanders formed a queue as they each offered a remorseful handshake.

But Grandad was not the type to hold a grudge.

Wait, hang on. Grandad was exactly the type to hold a grudge, and he looked down upon them all from that day forward (and not just from a height).

As I say, Edgar moved into the lighthouse with Sam and Grandad. He did not have a beard like Myrtle, but he had the fluffiest ears a 10-year-old boy has ever had. He decided to go back to school, not as headmaster but as a pupil.

Grandad too decided to take a few classes, more to spend time with his younger old brother than to get a more rounded education, and the two sat at the back of the room firing cattle snot at the blackboard (such was the trend at the time). Such behaviour put Major Chase in an uncomfortable position, not knowing fully how to discipline his former employer (who had a false set of teeth and was immune to his new teacher's odd and terrifying punishments).

Speaking of discipline, Major Chase took on the role of headmaster, although he continued on as Sam's teacher (and the island's dentist) such was his calling. The islanders agreed that, although Major Chase's dentistry techniques were old fashioned at best, and inhumane at worse, their children's grades had never been better, and their gum hygiene never healthier (although Weaver's two front teeth had *still* not arrived back from the mainland).

The children's parents now accepted that perhaps the monsters' banishment was not as final as it had once been believed. They finally believed in their existence ('About blooming time!', you cry) and followed Grandad's tricks of the trade: keeping their homes stocked with fire, laughter, nicknames, and, of course, jam.

Despite Sam and Grandad's searches, they never found Myrtle. Although they searched longingly for their friend, they knew she was gone forever. Still, sometimes at night, after Bedtime Supper (but before their nightly burping), if they listened really, really carefully, they were certain that they could hear the goat's majestic shouts swirl in through the lighthouse's cracks and crevasses.

And as for Sam, well, she slept soundly for the first time on Draymur Isle, her mother's snow globe on her bedside table and two very special granddads to watch over her.

* * *

I'll finish where I started.

There is a world under the bed that is as real as yours or mine.

It is a world of magic, both good and bad.

It is a world so different to our own, yet so similar at the same time.

I hope, Dear Reader, that you are still with me and that all your fingers, and thumbs, and toes, and toenails (and indeed your shoes) are all accounted for, and that you do now believe in these monsters.

And if you don't mind, if it's not too much trouble, you might do me the favour of yelling for all to hear . . .

MONSTERS UNDER THE BED ARE REAL!

ACKNOWLEDGEMENTS

I wish to thank all at HarperCollins Ireland, in particular my publisher, Conor Nagle, commissioning editor, Catherine Gough, and assistant editor, Kerri Ward, for their wisdom and support; my copy editor, Michelle Griffin, for her attention to detail; my enormously talented illustrator, Helen O'Higgins, for helping to bring the characters to life; my great friend, Robert Crowley, for his open ears; my family for their unending support.

Above all, I would like to thank my phenomenal wife, Zelda, for your love, enthusiasm and encouragement, and our darling son, Rafe, for the joy that you give us each and every day.